THE TRUFFLE WITH WEDDINGS

Annabelle Archer Wedding Planner Mystery #12

LAURA DURHAM

Broadmoor Books

❧ I ❧

"That's the last of it, Annabelle," my assistant Kate said as she carried a cardboard box into my apartment and dropped it on the floor with a thud. "I'm just sad we have to carry it all back down again in a few days."

"It may only be candy, but I still don't think it's safe to leave it in your car until the wedding on Saturday." I eyed the collection of white cardboard boxes now scattered around my living room floor and rubbed my arms for warmth after carrying boxes in from outside.

She sank onto my yellow overstuffed couch and relaxed her head so her blond bob draped over the back. "It's not like it was going to melt. First of all, it's February and it's below freezing out there, and secondly, it's all hard candies." She pulled her head up and grinned. "Wait a second. Did we order gummies for them?"

"If gummies come in all red or all pink, then we ordered them." It wasn't long ago that I'd placed the order for about twenty different varieties of pink and red candies to be displayed on our client's "candy bar"--everything from Twizzlers to giant baby-pink gumballs to Red Hots to strawberry-flavored rock candy.

As the owner of Wedding Belles, one of Washington, DC's top

wedding planning companies, I'd put together my fair share of candy displays. Despite being a fad that had come into fashion years ago, brides and grooms still loved having a table covered with giant glass apothecary jars filled with candies for guests to scoop into bags and take home as favors--even if Kate and I had grown weary of it. The only upside, as Kate saw it, was when the clients stocked their display with gummy bears, which were her go-to wedding day snack, and the thing that gave both of us the needed sugar boost to make it through the reception.

She sat forward and began nudging the boxes with the toe of her black high-heeled boot, squinting at the labels on the side. "Please tell me they got the Haribo Happy Cherries."

I sighed as I headed for the kitchen and the cup of coffee I'd abandoned when Kate arrived. "Somehow I don't think cherries scream 'love' enough for Amelia."

"I'm going to scream something before this wedding is over, and it's not going to be about love," Kate grumbled. "I mean, I get it. Valentine's-themed wedding the day before February 14th. You don't pick that date unless you're either obsessed with the holiday or enjoy paying twice as much for your flowers. Do I smell coffee?"

I peered over the open divider between my living room and galley kitchen, took a sip of my now lukewarm mocha-flavored coffee, and filled a mug for Kate from my French press. "I thought Valentine's Day was your holiday. Isn't Cupid your patron saint?"

Kate laughed. "Far from it. Cupid's known for his arrow hitting the mark. I, for one, am too young to settle down with just one guy. Not that it isn't great for some people."

I walked back into the living room and handed her a steaming mug of coffee. "Subtle. Real subtle." I knew she meant me and my boyfriend, Detective Mike Reese. He'd moved in a couple of months earlier, and I was still adjusting to the fact that I had a serious boyfriend and one that never left. "I thought you liked Reese."

Kate sipped her coffee, her hands wrapped around the sides of the mug for warmth. "I do. He's great." She glanced around the room, her eyes catching on one of his blazers slung across a dining room chair and a *Sports Illustrated* open on the glass-topped coffee table. "I don't know if I'd be able to narrow my field down to one."

Kate had always enjoyed an active social life, and I'd long since given up trying to keep track of the men she dated. I took the upholstered chair across from her, tucking my feet up under me. "How large of a field are we talking?"

She wagged an eyebrow at me. "So far I have three dates for Valentine's Day."

I almost choked on my coffee. "Three? On one day?"

"Don't look at me like that." She sat forward and put her mug down. "It may have gotten a little out of hand, but Fern's promised to help me manage it."

"How reassuring," I said, letting the sarcasm drip from my voice. Fern was our friend and go-to hairdresser who dolled-up all of our brides on their wedding days. He was known for precision cuts, meticulously themed outfits, and statement jewelry. He was not known for lowering the stress level of any situation, so I couldn't imagine how he would make juggling three dates anything less than a circus.

"I just hope I have the energy for three dates in a row after our wedding. What time do we end again on Saturday?"

"Midnight," I said. "The usual. Unless the bride decides to extend."

Kate held her fingers up to make air quotes. "I'm sure she will, because everything will be 'Ah-mazing.'"

We'd dubbed our Valentine's Day bride 'Ah-mazing Ah-melia' because she declared everything to be amazing and spoke like an Instagram caption complete with hashtags.

"Enough about my Valentine's plans," Kate said. "What do you and hottie cop have on the books for your first official V-D?"

Leave it to Kate to make the Hallmark holiday sound like something salacious. I felt my cheeks warm and brought my mug to my lips to cover them. "We haven't talked about it. I'm sure we'll do something low-key here."

Kate's eyes opened wide. "Are you telling me you haven't gotten anything for him yet? No card? No tasteful lingerie? No edible underwear?" She tapped her wrist even though she wore no watch. "Ticktock, Annabelle. It's already Tuesday. Less than a week to go. You don't want to be stuck digging through the dregs of the kinky underwear bin."

"What? No, of course not. What kinky underwear bin?" I held up a palm. "Never mind. I don't want to know." I instinctively looked toward the door, glad no one could hear through the thick walls of my old apartment building. "Do I need to remind you that Valentine's Day is about love and romance?"

"I wish you did. I feel like I've had about as much Valentine's Day romance as I can handle by planning Ah-melia's wedding. It's been nine months of tracking down cupid wings for flower girls and doves that can fly in heart-shaped formations. I am over it."

I knew what she meant. The bride had gone all-in on her theme, and I was feeling the Saint Valentine saturation myself. Maybe that was why I'd been putting off discussing plans with Reese. It felt strange to talk about romance when I planned it for a living. Of course, that didn't explain why he hadn't mentioned anything. I hoped he wasn't one of those men who refused to celebrate the holiday on the principle that it was a made-up day to sell cards and candy.

"Only a few more days," I said, holding up my mug in salute, "and we won't have to see anything red or heart shaped for a while."

Before I could take a drink, my door flew open and Richard staggered in holding two large white shopping bags. As he set the bags on the floor, a red heart-shaped box tumbled out of one and onto the rug covering my hardwoods.

"Et tu, Brutus?" I asked as my best friend and arguably the city's best caterer, Richard Gerard, unwound the gray cashmere scarf from his neck to reveal a pristine three-button suit in the same shade of gray with a pale-pink shirt and a gray tie.

"Are you two still sitting around gabbing?" He shook his head. "Some of us have been out making deliveries since nine o'clock."

Kate peered at the clock on my wall. "It's only ten, and since when do you make deliveries?"

I angled my head at him. "Kate's right. Don't you have a terrified and beleaguered staff who do that for you?"

Richard narrowed his eyes at both of us as he bent to pick up the box. "I make deliveries when I'm going for the personal touch. You know I need to drum up more business after I was blackballed from the list."

The list Richard referred to was the "Best Of" list that came out in *Capital Weddings* magazine's January issue. Richard Gerard Catering had been on the list every year and had often received the "top vote getter" star beside its name, but this year he had been left off completely. Richard had not taken it well.

Kate leaned over to get a better look at the box in his hands. "So you're giving Valentine's Day bribes?"

"Gifts," he said, smoothing the tag attached to the box. "A custom selection of gourmet chocolates from Fleurir."

"How many of those do you have in there?" Kate asked.

Richard touched a hand to his dark choppy hair. "Enough for every event venue in the city." His eyes darted to me. "And Annabelle convinced me to add one for the editor at *Capital Weddings*. I delivered that one yesterday."

I stood up with my mug and headed for the kitchen, squeezing his arm as I passed him. "I told you the editor was nice. Did you get to see Marcie when you dropped it off?"

Richard nodded. "For a moment, and she was perfectly polite. At least that horrible Marcus wasn't anywhere in sight."

Richard had once fired Marcus, who had then gone on to work at *Capital Weddings*. Richard suspected Marcus was behind him being removed from the "Best Of" list as an act of revenge.

"I'll bet she fired him," Kate said. "She didn't seem happy with him the last time we were there."

"She probably wasn't happy in general because we made such a scene," I called over my shoulder as I set my mug in the kitchen sink. Actually, Richard had been the one to make the scene, but I didn't want to call him out on it.

"Well, you can ask her when you see her at Love Brunch today," Richard said. "She mentioned yesterday she was attending. And you know who else I saw when I was at her offices? Brianna from Brides by Brianna." He wrinkled his nose. "Probably trying to toady up and get on the list. Tragic really."

I didn't point out he was doing the exact thing, as I knew he would not appreciate being compared to one of the newbie planners he considered a ditzy upstart. I peeked my head through the open space between the kitchen and living room. "Don't you mean Love Lunch?"

"Nope." Richard pulled back the French cuffs of his shirt to reveal his ever-present Cartier watch. "This year it's a brunch. It starts in an hour."

"What?" I rushed out of the kitchen. "Why didn't you say something earlier when you noticed me wearing leggings and a ratty sweater?"

Richard blinked and gave me the once-over. "I thought it was one of those shapeless sweater dress creations you tend to favor, darling."

I groaned and took off for my bedroom.

"Don't forget the color we're all supposed to wear this year is pink," Kate yelled.

This holiday was going to be the death of me.

2

Kate swung her car into the circular driveway in front of The Hay-Adams hotel, the vehicle jolting as she threw it into park when we reached the stone-columned portico. "Voila, and in record time too."

I shot a look over my shoulder to make sure I didn't see blue lights flashing. "And you only broke about a dozen traffic laws doing it."

"You know what they say." Kate winked at me. "The ends justify the memes."

"No one says that," I muttered to nobody but myself.

She stepped out of the car and handed her keys to the attendant, hooking her pink Kate Spade purse over her arm and walking around to meet me. "I have to tell you, Annabelle. I'm surprised by your outfit."

"Really?" I unbuttoned my coat so I could tug the hemline of my sweater dress down and wished the dress code for the event was any color other than pink. The only pink item that had also happened to be clean in my closet was a hot-pink sweater dress I'd accidentally sent through the wash, making it too tight and too short. The black boots I'd paired it with only covered my calves, leaving a significant amount of exposed leg--something I was used to seeing on Kate, not myself. I sucked in my stomach and wished the angora had more give. I felt like an itchy stuffed sausage.

"I'm surprised I like it," she said as we walked through the heavy wooden front doors held open by two attendants in black wool coats adorned with brass buttons and stripes on the cuffs. "You don't usually wear outfits that say 'look at me.'"

"I think this outfit is screaming 'save me.'" I hurried across the small lobby, not letting my eyes get drawn up to the high ceilings with ornate detailing or the rich wood-paneled walls. I registered the massive arrangement of white lilies and hydrangea on the table in front of the elevator bank and wondered if our florist friends Buster and Mack had designed it.

Even though I could smell the lingering scent of coffee from the first-floor restaurant, I ignored the short staircase leading up to it and darted down the alcove that held the express elevator. I pressed the call button and waited for Kate to catch up.

"I thought that was you scooting through the lobby, but I saw a flash of pink and thought it couldn't be Annabelle Archer," Fern said as he poked his head around the corner, his dark hair pulled up into a neat man bun. "But there you are. In pink."

"Don't you like it?" Kate asked as she linked her arm with his, and the two joined me in front of the elevator.

"It's so sassy. Are you sure it's not Kate's?"

"I wish," Kate and I said at the same time.

Fern giggled and smoothed the front of the baby-pink jacket that fit snugly across his chest and hugged his hips. A pink pocket square dotted with red hearts was perfectly folded into his lapel and matched the ascot billowing around his neck. An enormous garnet pin sparkled at his throat. Our friend and wedding hair guru took the concept of dressing for the occasion to the next level, and I felt relieved he wasn't wearing a pair of cupid wings attached to his jacket.

The elevator doors opened and I stepped inside, pressing the button for the rooftop. "It's always great to see you, but I thought this party was only for wedding planners."

Fern motioned to the small black-wheeled suitcase he pulled behind him. "The hotel catering execs wanted me to doll them up for the party. It's their big event of the year, you know."

That made sense. The Hay-Adams Valentine's Day party, or Love Brunch, was one of the must-attend events of the year. Guests had been known to buy special outfits, get blowouts, and have their makeup professionally done. Of course, I'd done none of these things. I tried not to think about the outfit I'd thrown on or the fact that I'd swiped on little more than blush and mascara before running out the door.

"Have you seen Buster and Mack?" I asked as the doors pinged open. "They were supposed to be doing all the decor."

"Is this your answer?" Kate asked as we stepped out of the elevator and into what appeared to be a forest complete with grass under our feet. Ceiling-high trees flanked the elevator with strands of pink orchids draped from the branches to the floor.

"Welcome to Love Brunch," a brunette with a breathy voice said, pushing aside the curtain of orchids with one hand and pointing down the wooded hall with the other. "The Queen of Hearts invites you to join her for cocktails."

"I think this is a take on *Alice in Wonderland*," I whispered to Kate and Fern as I pulled the heels of my boots out of the grass and followed the woman's direction. "That explains why Buster was talking about making giant toadstools."

We walked through the doorway, and I paused to take it all in. The walls had been draped in pink, and life-size playing cards adorned with red hearts were suspended from the ceiling. Several women dressed in red-and-black Queen of Hearts costumes strolled through the crowd, holding trays of cocktails. One of them paused and held out her tray to us.

"Isn't this darling?" Fern said as he took one of the pink-filled goblets with a tag around the stem that read, "Drink Me."

I took a glass and eyed the contents. "As long as it doesn't shrink my dress."

"I wouldn't mind a drink that shrinks me," Fern said, patting a hand to his flat stomach. "Too many temptations on Valentine's Day."

Kate leaned close to me. "Who do we like in this crowd?"

Fern took a sip of his cocktail and nodded his head toward a middle-aged buxom blonde. "Bambie Sitwell nabbed herself another rich husband, so don't get too attached to this face. She'll probably look different the next time we see her."

Kate shook her head. "You really think Boob Job Bambie will get more plastic surgery?"

Fern nudged us. "She's coming this way, and I can't tell if she's surprised to see us or if it's the eye lift."

"Annabelle! Kate!" She gave us air kisses when she reached us, then gave one to Fern. "Fernando!"

I knew Fern hated to be called by his given name--a by-product of his mother being an Abba fan--so I didn't need to look at his face to know he wasn't happy. Before he could make a snippy comment back, I put a hand on Bambie's arm. "Isn't this decor spectacular? You know Buster and Mack from Lush did all of this."

She nodded and attempted to smile, which made her look a little like the Joker from *Batman*. "I was just telling them how much I love the grass carpeting."

"Where are the dears?" Fern asked, craning his head around Bambie and scanning the mostly female and mostly pink crowd.

"It shouldn't be too hard to find two three-hundred-pound men in black leather," Kate said, flicking her hair off her face with a pink lacquered fingernail.

I spun around as I heard the sound of chains jingling over the conversation. One advantage of having friends who wore biker gear with lots of metal--it was easy to hear them approaching.

Mack reached me first and pulled me into a bear hug, his dark red goatee brushing my forehead. His eyes looked bloodshot, although I wasn't sure if it was from the intense decor installation for the brunch, or because they were now pseudo parents to a baby girl. The other half of the floral design duo who had dubbed themselves the Mighty Morphin Flower Arrangers, Buster lumbered up behind Mack--his black riding goggles pushed onto the top of his bald head--and gave us a weak smile. The matching dark circles under his eyes told me that whatever the reason, my friends weren't getting much sleep.

"You've outdone yourselves, boys," Fern said, waving a hand at the room and sloshing a bit of pink cocktail onto the grass carpet.

Buster gave a half shrug. "You know we love working at The Hay. We wanted to do something special for their event of the season."

I leaned close to Mack. "You look exhausted. Is it the party or the baby?"

Mack raised a pierced eyebrow. "We're used to big events. We're not used to midnight feedings."

I patted his thick forearm. "I thought things would be easier now that Merry and her mother live in the apartment over your shop."

Buster shifted from one foot to the other, and his leather pants creaked. "Prue is finishing up high school. That was the deal with her getting the apartment. We're trying to make sure she gets enough sleep, so Mack and I take Merry some nights."

Despite looking like Hell's Angels, my florist friends were softer than a pair of marshmallows. Mack pulled out his phone. "Do you want to see pictures?"

Kate, Fern, and I crowded around Mack so we could "ooh" and "aah" over the latest images of the baby.

"Not this again," Richard said with a sigh as he joined our group. "How is it that none of us are married, yet we're sharing baby photos?"

I elbowed him. "Stop it. You know you love Merry."

"I'll love it when she's out of the spitting-up phase." Richard brushed imaginary lint off his suit. "Babies and couture do not mix."

"Ignore him," Kate said to Mack. "He felt the same way about dogs, and now he carries his Yorkie around in a pocketbook."

Richard pursed his lips and glared at her. "If I've told you once, I've told you a thousand times. It's a man bag." His eyes slid to me and he blinked hard. "A sweater dress, darling? Really?"

I felt a flush creeping up my neck as I tugged at the hem of the dress. "It was the only thing pink in my closet, and I'll be burning it the second I get home."

"I'll spot you the matches," Richard muttered and turned to face the crowd. "Now, who do we love, and who are we trying to avoid?"

Fern lowered his voice. "There's Marcie from *Capital Weddings* magazine."

I followed his line of sight and spotted the tall woman with ebony hair standing next to one of the tree planters and inspecting the fluffy dried moss bunched around the base. "She's brave to make an appearance."

"Why do you say that?" Buster asked.

"This room is packed with people who either didn't make the "Best Of" list she curates and would sell their soul to get on, or people who made the list but are dying to get an "editor's pick" star by their name," I said. "Most of the magazine editors never come to events for that reason. It's a political minefield."

"Everyone either wants to hug her or kill her," Richard said. "Not that I would do either, mind you."

"Good," Kate let out a breath. "I, for one, would like to attend an event where someone doesn't leave in a body bag."

"Where's the fun in that?" Fern asked, downing the last of his cocktail in one gulp.

Kate clutched my arm. "Whatever you do, do not turn around."

3

I fought the urge to turn and see why Kate's eyes had gone so wide. "What? Who?" I gave an impatient sigh. "What are you talking about?"

Kate's face relaxed. "False alarm. I thought it was Brianna." She scanned the crowd. "Blond blowouts are a big thing today."

The owner of Brides by Brianna had hit the DC wedding scene a couple of years earlier with lots of her daddy's money, a Southern drawl that made her sound sweeter than she was, and almost no experience. Instead of making nice with us, she'd decided to spread rumors and try to tank our business. Since then, our encounters had not been pleasant.

"Don't do that." Richard fanned himself with a pink cocktail napkin. "You nearly made me spill my drink."

Fern's eyes twinkled as he smiled like the Cheshire Cat himself. "I'd love to see Brianna. The last time I saw her, she'd severely over plucked her eyebrows. I need to see if they grew back."

"I'm sure she's here somewhere, but there's no need to get worked up," I said. "It's not like she's going to bite us."

"She might pluck us," Fern said, giggling and putting a hand over his mouth.

I didn't acknowledge his comment or Kate joining in on the giggling. "Now I'm going to go over and say hello to Marcie."

Kate took a heart-shaped hors d'oeuvre off a passing tray and popped it into her mouth. "Right behind you, boss."

"While you're doing that," Fern said, his eyes darting over the sea of heads, "I'm going to go talk to the planner who needs to do her roots."

"I think that's a performer in a skunk costume," Kate told him, peering at his empty glass. "How many cocktails have you had?"

"Why?" Fern blinked rapidly. "You don't think they have alcohol, do you? They taste like strawberry punch."

Mack put a hand under Fern's arm. "Why don't we find him a nice toadstool to sit on?" He waved us away as he and Buster led Fern to a cluster of giant polka-dotted mushrooms. "We'll catch up to you later."

"Come on." I tugged Richard's arm. "This is the perfect time to ingratiate yourself with Marcie."

Richard shook off my hand and smoothed the arm of his jacket where I'd grabbed it. "I thought that's what I did yesterday with the box of chocolates."

I took a final sip of my berry-flavored cocktail and set the empty goblet down onto a table designed to look like a supersized teacup, then gave Richard a pointed look. "Do you want to get on the list again or not?"

"I think I liked you better when you were young and clueless and looked to me for advice, darling," Richard said. "Since when did you become the expert in strategy and wedding industry politics?"

"Right?" Kate leaned across me and gave Richard a knowing look. "I think you've created a monster."

I linked my arms through Kate's and Richard's and propelled them forward with me, muttering apologies as we parted the crowd. I blew a few air kisses and gave a few finger waves as we passed people I knew, but I didn't stop until we'd reached Marcie.

She smiled when she saw us and pulled her hand back from the trunk of one of the tall trees nestled in a massive terra-cotta planter. "I was seeing if the trees were real." She motioned up at the leafy canopy touching the ceiling and dripping with strands of orchids. "How many hours do you think it took to string all these orchids?"

"A lot," I said.

Marcie nodded her head at wall-sized frames that held three-dimensional "portraits" of pastoral scenes complete with real flowers and models protruding from the painting. "How did they get frames that large up here?"

"Well, it is an *Alice in Wonderland* theme," Kate said, catching a waiter by the arm, snagging two cocktails from his tray, and handing one to the willowy magazine editor. "Maybe they shrunk them."

Marcie laughed and shifted the large Tory Burch tote onto her shoulder as she took the cylindrical glass filled with bright-green liquid. "This is my first time at Love Brunch. I had no idea it was this elaborate."

"Buster and Mack have taken it to the next level," I said, taking a glass from the waiter's tray as well. "This event used to be a simple affair, but they decided to splash it out and make it the event of the season."

Marcie swept her eyes across the room, lingering on the far wall covered in gold-rimmed clock faces the size of hubcaps. "Mission accomplished."

"Some people just can't resist the dramatic," Richard said.

Bold words from a man who had a Burberry coat that matched his own for his dog.

"Valentine's Day is a big deal for the wedding industry," I explained. "Kate and I are working on a wedding for this weekend that's completely themed around the holiday. It's pretty intense."

"I think you mean crazy," Kate said in a mock whisper. "The flower girls actually have cupid wings."

"You should submit it to the magazine," Marcie said. "We're always looking to feature weddings with a creative twist." Her eyes went to Richard. "Speaking of creative, those chocolates you gave me are so unique. I'd never heard of wasabi truffles before. Or strawberry ginger."

Richard put a hand to his chest. "I wanted something memorable. Something that would remind people that Richard Gerard Catering is known for innovative cuisine." He gave his most simpering smile. "I hope you enjoyed them."

Marcie nodded a little too quickly. "Oh, I did."

A giant rabbit hopped by us ringing a silver bell and singing, "Don't be late for your very important brunch date."

"I think that means we're supposed to be seated," I said, noticing people beginning to move toward the doors leading into the main room.

We followed the flow and walked into the long rectangular ballroom overlooking the White House on one side. Aside from the wall of entirely glass-paned French doors, the room had been draped in sheer white fabric. A single long table extended from one end of the room to the other and was also draped in white gossamer with glossy black candlesticks and round arrangements of tightly packed white roses running down the middle. Long strips of black and white ribbons were suspended from the recessed ceiling over the table and nearly touched the floral arrangements.

I started to search for the cards at the top of the place settings that would indicate who sat where, but then realized the names were written in swirling black letters on the backs of the Plexiglas ghost chairs around the table.

"Here we are," Kate called from the other end of the table.

I marveled that she'd managed to move so much faster than me, especially since her shoes were significantly higher than mine. Scooting around to join her, I greeted several of my friendly competitors and paid appropriate compliments to their pink outfits, including to one planner who wore a pink tutu topped with a sequined sweater. If I'd thought Buster and Mack's decor was over-the-top, it was only because I hadn't seen all the outfits.

"It looks like someone knew what they were doing," Kate said when I'd reached her. "You and I are together and Richard is across from us. I don't think they put any of our frenemies near us."

I gestured for her to keep her voice down. "We don't have any frenemies."

"Okay, enemies then," Kate said. "It would be a long brunch if we had to sit next to Brianna."

I looked over my shoulder, hoping the blond planner with her sickly sweet Southern accent wasn't in sight. "Do you see her?"

"Luckily, no, although I do enjoy watching her turn purple every time she lays eyes on Fern."

In response to Brianna's unkind comments about Wedding Belles, Fern had made sure everyone who passed through his society hair salon thought Brianna's business was a front for a high-priced call girl service. This hadn't been true, but Fern considered turnabout fair play. Even though she'd vehemently denied the rumors, Brianna had never been able to completely shake the whispers or the scandal, and she'd never forgiven Fern although she couldn't prove he'd been the one to start the rumors in the first place. She'd never forgiven us for being his friends, and as she rightfully suspected, the reason he'd gone after her.

"I hope they're serving the oatmeal soufflé," I said as I pulled out my chair and took a seat next to Kate.

Kate picked up the black-and-white menu card. "You're in luck. It's the first course." She patted her stomach. "I'm glad I didn't eat breakfast so I'll have room for all these carbs."

Fern, looking very alert, sank into the chair next to me on the other side.

"What happened to you?" I asked.

"The boys just poured about a pot of coffee down my throat." He blinked hard as he looked around the room. "It seems to have worked. I don't see any giant toadstools or life-sized bunnies anymore."

Before I could explain to him that we were in a different room, my attention was drawn to the tinkling of silverware against glass. The hotel's director of catering, a petite brunette with Fern's signature smoky eyes, stood at the head of the table, holding up a glass of champagne.

"I'd like to welcome you all to the annual Love Brunch at the Top of the Hay." She beamed up and down the table. "Of course we couldn't do this event without the help of our incredible team. We're so grateful to Buster and Mack from Lush for the spectacular decor." She paused to clap and everyone joined her.

I craned my neck to look for the pair and spotted them at the other end of the table, smiling and looking embarrassed.

"And a special thank you to Brianna from Brides by Brianna for designing the menu cards and signage for us," the woman continued, inclining her head to a spot halfway down the table and raising her glass.

Kate and I both snapped our heads around and saw Brianna giving us what could only be described as an evil grin. I wouldn't have been surprised to see feathers sticking out of the corner of her mouth. How had she managed to worm her way into Love Brunch? The event had never had a planner involved before since it was an event for planners, and I'd always assumed they didn't want to be perceived as playing favorites. I attempted to catch Richard's eye across the table, but he'd plastered on his fakest smile as the planner next to him said something.

"Does she even do weddings here?" Kate whispered to me as everyone but the two of us and Fern drank sips of champagne in toast to Brianna.

I shrugged. "Who knows? I didn't think so, but you know how good she is at networking."

"If you can call giving out expensive gifts networking," Kate said, reaching for her champagne flute after the catering director sat down and the waiters had begun placing ramekins of oatmeal soufflé in front of guests. She swigged the entire glass and set it back down. "When are we going to give out designer clutches for holiday presents?"

I picked up my spoon and dipped it into the caramel-brown soufflé topped with powdered sugar, feeling the steam rise up from the inside. "When we get adopted by someone absurdly wealthy, I suppose."

"What I need to focus on is finding a rich sugar daddy." Kate waved her spoon at me. "That would solve all our problems."

Fern leaned over me and nodded. "Now you're talking. Annabelle is a lost cause since she's gone and fallen for a civil servant. " He winked at me. "He's hot, I'll give you that, sweetie, but now it's up to Kate to reel in a rich old man with a bad heart."

"Would you still work for me if you had a sugar daddy?" I asked, pausing with my spoon halfway to my mouth.

Kate squeezed my arm. "You know I would. I'd never want to miss all this fun."

I took a bite of the soufflé and closed my eyes as the flavors of cinnamon and warm blueberries mingled on my tongue. All the comfort of oatmeal with the lightness of a soufflé and the sweetness of a dessert. The dish really was heavenly.

"Speaking of Mr. Hunky," Fern nudged me and pointed to the door behind us, "did you tell him where you were going today?"

I twisted my head to see Reese and his partner standing in the doorway and whispering to the catering captain as they all pored over a diagram. Tall and dark haired, my cop boyfriend had muscles evident even in a blazer that was too boxy. I felt a flutter of butterflies in my stomach when I spotted him, especially since I knew how good he looked when he wasn't wearing a shapeless blazer and work pants. But what was he doing here? I knew he was working, and as much as I liked spending time with him, I sincerely hoped he wasn't here to see me.

Any suspicion of that was eliminated when he crossed the room and leaned over to Marcie.

"Is that Reese?" Kate asked me, her eyes going up and down the table. "What's he doing here? Did someone drop dead and I missed it?"

Marcie clamped her hand over her mouth and stood up so

quickly her chair flew behind her and hit one of the French doors with a clatter. "I can't believe it. That's not possible."

Murmurs passed through the room, and I heard the words "dead" and "poison."

"If you'll just come with us and answer a few questions." Reese tried to take her elbow and she shook him off.

"That's what I'm trying to tell you," Marcie said, her voice shrill. "The chocolates didn't come from me." She extended a finger in front of her. "They were from him."

Every head in the room swiveled to stare at Richard, whose mouth fell open as he dropped a spoonful of soufflé that splattered onto the table and sent droplets of oatmeal into his hair.

Marcie collapsed onto the floor with a sob. "He killed Marcus."

4

"**S**he threw me under the bus," Richard said as he wrung his hands and paced a small circle around a giant teacup. "How could she say I killed Marcus? And how can you be eating at a time like this?"

I paused with a spoonful of oatmeal soufflé halfway to my mouth. "You mean lunchtime?"

Richard rolled his eyes at me, but I continued to eat. By this point, I'd been involved with enough murder investigations to know we might be a while, and it was rare I got to eat the hotel's famous oatmeal soufflé. "Just because I'm chewing doesn't mean I'm not strategizing. I can multitask, you know."

"Then multitask us out of here." Richard dodged a giant playing card hanging from the ceiling. "I'm starting to feel like I really have fallen through a rabbit hole."

"I'm sure Reese will be back soon," I said. "Despite what she said, Marcie is the one they came here to talk to. I'm sure holding us is just a formality so they can eliminate us as suspects. They're probably talking to other planners too."

Richard gave me a look that told me he didn't believe a word I'd said. After the initial hysteria--mostly from Richard--we'd been separated from Marcie and the rest of the guests. The three of us had been shuffled off to the cocktail area, while Marcie had been taken to a meeting room where she could be questioned. It hadn't escaped me that Brianna had been the person comforting Marcie, and I wondered how well they knew each other.

Fern crossed his legs as he perched on a brightly colored toadstool. "Isn't Marcus the guy you fired?"

"Yes," Richard said. "But that was ages ago."

"But didn't you blame him for getting you kicked off the 'Best Of' list?" Fern asked, pumping his leg up and down.

"Not so loud," I whispered to Fern. "We don't need to gift wrap Richard's motives."

Richard narrowed his eyes at Fern. "Since when did you have a memory like a steel trap?"

"I've been doing online brain exercises," Fern told him. "They help me in the salon when I need to tell one blond socialite from the other. After a while all those bleached heads start to run together."

"The free-flowing champagne at the salon may have something to do with that," I muttered into my soufflé.

Richard rested one arm on a gigantic frame and draped the other over his forehead. "You don't think Reese will consider those actual motives, do you? I mean, this is all circumstantial. It's a wild coincidence."

I set my empty soufflé bowl down onto the nearest cocktail table draped in a black-and-white-checkerboard cloth. The themed cocktail room didn't seem as festive without people milling about, and I wished there were more of the fruity but deadly drinks at the now-empty bar to take the edge off Richard's escalating panic. I joined Fern on his toadstool and tugged at my hemline. It felt like my dress had drunk a 'shrink me' potion.

I ignored Richard's questions and his increasingly hysterical tone of voice. "I'm sure he'll weigh everything carefully. We don't know any details about Marcus's death yet."

"Poisoning," Kate said as she walked up and sat on the other side of Fern, crossing her ankles out in front of her and showing lots of bare leg.

I did a double take when I realized Kate had emerged from a cluster of uniformed cops in the hall. "I thought you went to the ladies' room."

She winked at me and then at one of the cops. "I took a little detour."

I decided not to take the time to lecture Kate on the number of detours currently in her life. Sometimes Kate's shameless flirting came in handy.

Richard looked out from under his arm. "Who said it was poison?"

Kate leaned back. "The police got a 9-1-1 call from *Capital Weddings* magazine earlier this morning reporting that someone had eaten a chocolate and dropped dead. When they got there, Marcus was DOA."

"So they're just assuming it's poison because the caller said he ate a chocolate and then died," I said. "They can't know for sure until they do a tox screening."

"Oo-hoo-hoo." Fern slapped my leg. "Look who knows all the lingo now that she's living with a detective. All that pillow talk really is paying off, sweetie."

Richard groaned. "Sleeping with the enemy, you mean."

"You know you like Reese," I said. "And he's not the enemy. He's actually the best chance you have of not being a suspect."

"Is that so?" Reese's voice startled me from behind. "Are you already handing out prison pardons on my behalf?"

"Prison?" I could barely hear Richard's wisp of a whimper.

"Don't tease him," I said as I stood. "You know he doesn't take things like this lightly."

"None of you should be taking this lightly," Reese said. "One of your colleagues was killed, potentially poisoned, and the most obvious method of poison seems to be the chocolates Richard delivered yesterday."

"I wouldn't call him a colleague," Kate said. "The only person here who met him more than once was Richard."

Richard shot her a look, but she didn't notice because she was making eyes at one of the cops.

"Is that true?" Reese glanced around our group of four. "You didn't regularly interact with the victim?"

"Capital Weddings may be a wedding magazine, but the people who work there don't usually socialize with our industry. I only recently met Marcie, the head editor, and I'll probably never lay eyes on all the assistants and interns who work there." I came around my chair to stand next to Reese. "I doubt anyone else at Love Brunch knew Marcus."

Reese pulled a small notepad out of his pocket and flipped a few pages. "So if Marcus wasn't really a part of your wedding planner crowd, why was he given a box of chocolates by Richard?"

"The chocolates weren't for him," Richard said. "They were a gift for Marcie. I can't believe she regifted them to her assistant. What is this world coming to?"

"So you gave Marcie a box of chocolates for Valentine's Day?" Reese looked up, a confused look on his face. "Were you two . . . close?"

Richard rolled his eyes. "I gave everyone chocolates. It was a marketing ploy to drum up business since Richard Gerard Catering had been cruelly left off the *Capital Weddings* 'Best Of' list. I had Fleurir put together an assortment in their red heart-shaped boxes, and I added a custom tag." He gave Reese a pointed look. "Fleurir is a high-end chocolatier for those of you not in the culinary loop."

"How many did you give out?" Reese asked.

Richard drummed his fingers on the handle of the supersized teacup. "At least twenty-five. I ordered thirty boxes to be sure I had extras in case I thought of someone last minute or had forgotten a venue."

"I'll need to get a list of everyone you gave them to," Reese said. "To make sure no other box was tainted."

"Of course." Richard fanned himself with one hand, no doubt feeling faint at the thought of other people dying at the hands of his gift. "Marcie won't be on the original list, though. She was actually one of the extras."

"You didn't initially plan to give one to her?"

"Not at all," Richard told him. "I was still miffed about the list, but Annabelle convinced me I should take the high road and give her one."

Reese closed his eyes for a second. "So giving the chocolates to Marcie was Annabelle's idea?"

"Yes," I said, "but I stand behind the decision. Richard was trying to get back on the list, and a gift is the perfect way to get noticed."

"So let me see if I understand," Fern said, waving his hands in the air and leveling a finger at Richard. "You gave the chocolates to Marcie who gave them to her assistant, who you despise, who ate one and died."

If looks could have killed, Richard's gaze would have struck down Fern instantly.

"Well, that seems like an awfully roundabout way to kill someone," Fern continued. "How could Richard have known any of that would happen?"

"That's a good point." Kate pulled her eyes away from the uniformed officers. "It doesn't make any sense."

"No it doesn't," Reese said, "which is why we're assuming Marcie was the intended victim all along. She already told us the chocolates were meant for her."

I put a hand to my mouth. "So someone managed to poison the chocolates in an attempt to kill Marcie, but she inadvertently saved herself by giving them away?"

"Talk about a good regift," Fern muttered.

Reese rocked back on his heels. "And as far as we can tell, they only poisoned the one chocolate Marcus ate, because he shared the box with the other assistants and no one else died or even got sick. Everyone we spoke to at the magazine confirmed he just ate the one truffle, and he'd complained earlier about not eating breakfast."

"What about coffee?" I suggested. "I'm sure he had coffee."

Reese shook his head. "An intern had gone over to Starbucks for everyone but returned after Marcus collapsed."

Kate grimaced. "So the guy is starving, and the first thing he eats kills him?"

"Talk about an efficient killer," I said. "They really knew what they were doing."

"Let's hope not," Reese reminded me, "because Marcie's still alive, and the killer is still out there."

≈ 5 ≈

I ducked inside the door to my stone-fronted apartment building, eager to escape the chill and pleased I'd snagged street parking only a block away. Parking in my fashionable Georgetown neighborhood was impossible to find, and it seemed like I spent a decent portion of my life searching for a space.

"Just the lady I was hoping to see." My elderly neighbor, Leatrice, leaned out of her first-floor apartment. Even though she must have been eighty--and didn't look a day over ninety--she hadn't lost a bit of her hearing. In fact, I usually crept upstairs barefoot to avoid being waylaid by her and her high-powered ears.

I put a hand to my heart. "I didn't see you there. Were you waiting in the doorway?"

Leatrice had a fondness for true crime and had even gone so far as to get her own police scanner, so I braced myself for a barrage of questions about the murder. Even though she wouldn't know the connection to Richard, she'd know my boyfriend was involved.

She laughed and touched a hand to her unnaturally dark flipped-up hair. "Don't be silly, dear. I was decorating my door when you came in."

Apparently, she'd missed the report of the homicide in the

midst of decorating. Her wooden door was indeed covered with red paper hearts embellished with paper doilies, and I noticed her pink sweatpants had "Hot Stuff" written down one leg in red. "You're getting in the Valentine's Day spirit."

"It's the first Valentine's Day in decades where I've actually had a sweetheart." A wide smile spread across her wrinkled face. "Sidney Allen and I are going all out."

I stifled a groan. Leatrice had met the excitable entertainment designer at one of my weddings, and the two had been inseparable ever since. It wasn't that I disliked Sidney Allen with his double name--woe to the person who dared to use only one--and his insistence on wearing a headset and his pants hiked up around his armpits; he was just a lot to handle. Combine that with Leatrice's non-stop energy and creative clothing, and it could drive the most devoted teetotaler to drink.

"What are you and the adorable detective doing for Valentine's Day?" she asked.

This again. I gave what I hoped sounded like a breezy laugh. "I'm not sure yet. I haven't given it too much thought since Kate and I have a big wedding coming up on Saturday."

"You wouldn't be interested in joining us, would you?"

I knew from previous discussions that Reese would rather go on a double date with Richard and his dog than with Leatrice and Sidney Allen. "That's so sweet, but we wouldn't want to intrude."

"A wedding the day before Valentine's Day." Leatrice clapped her hands together. "How romantic. I'm assuming the bride is using the holiday as her theme?"

"And then some," I said. "It's her favorite holiday, and she's gone a little overboard with the pink and red."

"Well, I hope you and your beau get to do something special on Sunday, even if you will be exhausted. It's your first Valentine's Day together, too, isn't it?"

I started up the stairs, hoping to escape what felt like the third degree. If anyone else asked me about my Valentine's Day plans, I was going to break out in hives. "I'm sure we'll think of something."

Leatrice began to follow me, so I turned and thrust a round box at her. "Why don't you enjoy these? They're heart-shaped cookies from the brunch I came from."

"Don't you want them?"

I touched a hand to my stomach. "I've had too much sugar already, but I'd hate for them to go to waste."

"Wait," Leatrice said. "I almost forgot. I accepted a delivery for you while you were out." She dashed back into her apartment and returned with a dark-brown box tied with a pink ribbon. "The delivery man said they were from a caterer."

I peered at the box and the logo on the top of the card. A rival catering company must be trying to woo my business away from Richard with a Valentine's Day gift. "Thanks for holding them for me."

"Aren't you going to open it?"

I hurried up the next few steps until I reached the first landing. "I'm sure it's cookies or some other Valentine's Day treats. A lot of wedding vendors send out treats this week."

Leatrice pressed her hands together. "Of course. Weddings, love, Valentine's Day."

"Something like that," I said. More like marketing, leads, bookings, but I didn't want to burst her bubble. "I have to go return a bunch of phone calls, but I'll see you later."

I gave a backward wave as I continued up the stairs, not stopping until I'd reached my fourth-floor apartment. After pushing open the door, I dropped my keys into the bowl on the nearby bookshelf and flopped down onto my couch. Between rushing out the door in the morning and the shock of the murder, I was worn out. Even though I enjoyed living with Reese, I was glad to have the place to myself. I didn't even mind that Kate had gone off on a coffee date with one of the uniformed officers instead of coming back with me to the office.

I tossed the brown box onto the cushion next to me and let my head drop back as I closed my eyes and soaked in the quiet. I didn't even hear street sounds since I was on the top floor and kept my windows closed. A hard pounding made me jerk up.

"Annabelle, you have to let me in!"

I answered the door, and Richard rushed inside.

"Are they behind me?" he asked from the other side of the room, clutching his brown-and-black Yorkie, Hermes, under his arm.

I peeked into the hall. It was empty. "Is who behind you?"

"The paparazzi," he said, setting Hermes onto the couch. "I'm sure they were following me when I left my place."

I watched Hermes run back and forth on the couch, his tiny pink nose sniffing the surface and then inspecting the round box. He looked almost as nervous as his owner. "Back up a second. Why would paparazzi be following you? Wait. Do we even have paparazzi in DC?"

"Of course we do." Richard cut his eyes to me. "I think they have to have second jobs, but we have them."

I closed the door and headed for the kitchen. "And they would be chasing you because . . .?"

Richard let out a deep sigh. "Really, Annabelle. I'd think it would be obvious. Someone leaked to the press that I was implicated in a murder."

I took two bottles of water from the fridge and walked back into the living room, handing Richard one and reclaiming my spot on the couch as he paced in front of my windows. "Impossible. The murder just happened. I don't think the police have even filed all their reports yet."

"Then it must have been an inside job." He spun around to face me. "How much do you really know about this Reese fellow?"

"Enough to know he wants to deal with a hysterical version of you about as much as I do."

Richard paused for a moment. "You may be right. He doesn't seem the type to leak to the press." He sucked in a quick breath. "I'll bet it's that loon downstairs."

"Leatrice?" I shook my head while Hermes yipped at the name. "First of all, she's not a loon. She just likes unique clothing and spying on her neighbors. If she's so crazy, why do you let her babysit your dog all the time?"

Richard glanced at his dog. "To be honest, he's a bit of a N-U-T himself."

"Did you just spell in front of the dog?" I asked.

"You'd be surprised how much he understands, darling. Thankfully I know kitchen Spanish from my cooks; otherwise I wouldn't be able to talk about menus at all in front of him. He doesn't understand 'pollo' yet but say the word C-H-I-C-K-E-N and he goes crazy. "

I looked down at Hermes, who was splayed out next to me, his silky ears tilted up like he was listening. "Are you telling me I need to learn Spanish to have a normal conversation in front of your dog?"

He shrugged. "It wouldn't hurt. How fast can you spell out loud?"

I ignored his question. "Leatrice couldn't have told anyone about the murder because she doesn't know. I saw her a few minutes ago and she didn't say a word. You know she would have mentioned it if she'd heard on her scanner. Are you sure the paparazzi were following you?"

Richard walked over to the window facing the street and pulled back the yellow twill curtain. "I could have sworn I saw someone suspicious looking when I drove up to my building." He scanned from left to right. "Okay, I might have been wrong about the paparazzi, but this is still a catastrophe."

"Might I remind you we've been here before? We've both been a suspect in a murder case and we survived."

Richard dug into the leather bag he wore over one shoulder and produced the box of cookies from the brunch. "This is different."

"You're right. The other times we had more motive and opportunity." I watched with some concern as Richard opened the box and bit into an iced, heart-shaped cookie. "Since when do you eat sugar in the middle of the day?"

"Since it doesn't matter if I'm bloated from carbs," he said, crumbs spilling from his mouth. "Who cares what I look like if I'm ruined?"

I stood and took the box of cookies from Richard. "You aren't ruined. This is all a big mistake. Like the others."

"The other times I was at the top of my game. I was on 'the list' as one of DC's top caterers. I was in demand." His voice cracked. "This is different. I've fallen off the list, and business is already down. Those chocolates were supposed to remind people that Richard Gerard Catering stands for innovation and excellence. Instead, they turned out to be the instrument of my demise."

As he collapsed onto a chair with a wail, I wondered if--although overly dramatic, per usual--he might also be right. No one would forget a caterer who gave out poisoned chocolates for Valentine's Day.

❦ 6 ❦

"**A**re you sure about this?" I asked from the kitchen doorway as I watched Richard bustle around my narrow kitchen, moving effortlessly from the refrigerator to the stove as he assembled ingredients on the countertop.

Richard looked up at me, a white apron tied around his neck. "You know cooking calms me, darling."

The scent of coffee from the morning had been replaced by the smell of caramelizing onions sizzling in a sauté pan. It was rare my kitchen smelled like anything other than coffee or toast, although I'd been telling myself I should learn to cook since Reese had moved in. Not that he complained. Since he'd been living on takeout for years, my meager skills in the kitchen were not a sticking point.

"Only if you're sure," I said. "I don't want you to feel like you have to sing for your supper."

Richard waved a wooden spoon at me. "Nonsense. Hermes and I can't exactly ask for asylum without doing something to contribute."

My efforts to convince Richard he was safe from the media hadn't been completely successful, and he'd claimed to be too wrung out to trudge home with Hermes in tow. I wasn't sure what Reese would think about all this when he came home from work.

"And you don't need my help?" I asked.

"Annabelle, please." Richard handed me a glass of white wine. "You know I adore you, but you're a bit of a disaster in the kitchen."

I thought disaster was a strong word, but I took the glass of wine and let him shoo me out of the room. I sat next to Hermes on the couch, tucking my feet up under me and feeling glad I'd changed back into leggings and a sweater. I set my wine on the coffee table and checked my phone. Nothing from Reese--not a surprise since he was busy with a case--and a short message from Kate saying she'd see me in the morning. I texted her back a "thumbs-up" emoji and felt pleased with myself for learning the language of the millennial generation.

Hermes sniffed my wine when I lifted the glass to take a sip, shook his head as if disgusted by the smell, and curled up in a silky ball beside me. I knew the wine in my fridge was only a baby step up from "Two Buck Chuck" wine from Trader Joe's, and I suspected Richard had trained the little dog to be as much of a snob as he was. "Good thing you're both cute," I whispered to him, petting his head.

I looked at the screen of my phone. I should give Reese some warning about what he was walking into.

Coming home soon? I typed and watched the question appear in a green talk bubble.

The blinking dots at the bottom of the screen told me he was typing a reply. *On my way.*

How close?

A pause before the blinking dots appeared. *Why?*

Drat. He was on to me. One of the problems with dating a detective--it was hard to slip things by him. *I hope you're in the mood for a gourmet dinner.*

A long pause while he typed. *I hope you're kidding.*

I left my phone on the couch as I ducked into the kitchen to grab one of Reese's favorite microbrews, twisting the cap off and heading back for the front door as I heard the keys jingling in the lock. I met him in the doorway and handed him the beer.

He looked at me, then the bottle, and peered over my head to Richard in the kitchen. He dropped his worn leather satchel on the floor and took a long swig.

"I can explain," I said.

He put a finger to my lips and pulled me close to him with his other arm and bent down to kiss me. Not a quick peck, either. I felt the kiss all the way to my toes and was dazed when he finally released me. His hazel eyes had deepened to green, and one errant dark curl dipped down onto his forehead. Now *I* wished Richard was anywhere but in my kitchen.

"Honey, I'm home," Reese called out when he released me and took a few more steps into our apartment.

Richard's head appeared over the divider between the kitchen and living room. "Dinner will be ready shortly, Detective." He pointed his spoon at me. "Annabelle, would you be a doll and clear the dining table?"

I glanced over at the table I used as a catchall for papers, client files, and magazines. I knew Richard would not go for balancing plates on knees since Reese was here.

"Let me help," my boyfriend said as he came up behind me.

I started to protest. "You don't know which papers go--"

He slid everything off the table and into his arms, then walked it over to the overstuffed chair and deposited it.

"Thanks." I tried not to cringe thinking of all the papers mixed up together. Served me right for leaving it out for so long.

Richard pushed me aside as he set three neatly folded napkins and the accompanying silverware around the table, and hurried back to the kitchen.

I eyed the yellow chevron patterned cloth napkins. "Where did you find these?"

"I brought them here months ago, of course," Richard called

back. "I knew you relied on that absurd stash of paper take-out napkins, and as you are fully aware, I don't do paper."

"Oh, I'm aware." Before I could wonder what other things Richard had hidden around the apartment, he returned with three plates stacked waiter style up one arm and set them on the table.

"It smells great." Reese pulled out a chair and sat down.

Richard gave a quick smile. "As you can imagine, I had very little to work with and no time to go shopping, so it's a simple pasta dish with a light cream sauce and strips of prosciutto."

I stared at the pretty swirls of angel hair pasta dotted with the paper-thin Italian ham. "I've never bought prosciutto, or is that another thing you stashed here without my knowledge?"

Richard fluttered a hand at me. "Only a few essentials, darling. The real crime is that you've never bought prosciutto."

Richard was probably the only person I knew who considered gourmet ham to be an essential, I thought as I sat down next to Reese and unfurled the napkin over my lap.

My boyfriend took a bite, closing his eyes for a moment as he chewed and swallowed. He turned to Richard. "When do you move in?"

Richard flushed from the compliment and twirled his own forkful of pasta. "I'm only here because I was chased out of my place by the paparazzi. Well, one paparazzi. Is that called a paparazzo?"

"There was a photographer outside your building?" Reese asked.

"He thinks," I said. "He can't be sure, and I told him there was no way a cop leaked any information about the case."

I took a bite and marveled at what Richard had done with so few ingredients. The sauce was light with just enough rich prosciutto flavor, and the pasta was perfectly cooked. I did miss Richard's kitchen invasions, which had been few and far between since I'd "shacked up with another man," as he liked to put it.

Reese picked up his bottle of pale ale. "There's not much to leak, and I can't see why someone would since it isn't a high-profile case."

Richard pulled himself to his full height. "'Caterer to the rich and powerful offs enemy with poisoned chocolate right before Valentine's Day?' The headline writes itself, Detective."

"Never be your own lawyer," Reese said and took a long drink.

"I don't know how you can even be sure the murder weapon was the poisoned chocolate," I said. "We're only assuming that because the person who called 9-1-1 said he died after eating it. Marcus could have ingested the poison earlier, and the murder could have nothing to do with Richard's chocolates."

"He could have been poisoned by something else, but he wasn't." Reese took another bite and swallowed. "I shouldn't tell you this, but since Richard saved me from pizza delivery, I will. The ME was able to pump the victim's stomach. There was nothing in there but chocolate, although a larger amount than you'd expect from one truffle. I suspect he ate more than one and the witnesses didn't notice or forgot. Eyewitnesses are notoriously unreliable."

Richard's fork clattered to the table, his expression stricken.

I put a hand over his and turned to Reese. "For your information, I was not going to order pizza."

He grinned at me. "I like pizza, babe. I like this more, but you know I don't mind takeout."

"Could we please focus?" Richard said. "On me? You two will have plenty of time to complain about Annabelle's lack of cooking skills after I'm carted off to prison."

I took my hand off his. "If I were you, I wouldn't alienate my friends. Who else do think is going to bake a nail file into a cake for you?"

Richard gave a strangled cry and put a hand to his cheek. "I'm doomed. Do you even know how to bake a cake?"

"This Marcus fellow may have been your arch enemy, but as I mentioned earlier, it doesn't seem like he was the target." Reese looked unconcerned as he ate another forkful of pasta. "Did you have a motive to kill Marcie?"

"Not really," Richard said. "She was the editor of the magazine that had knocked me off its list, but with that logic any vendor in DC who didn't make the list or was kicked off could have done it. I wasn't the only person to be removed this year, you know."

I hadn't known. I'd been so focused on Richard not making the list, and on Wedding Belles getting the 'top vote getter' star, I hadn't paid much attention to the other names. "Who else got kicked off?"

"Petals and Petunias for one." Richard held up his fingers and began counting them off. "That cheesy band agent Ron Twinkle, I think his real last name is Tinker, and Skyfall Video. There may be more I'm not thinking about. Not to mention all the people who try to get on the list by wooing the editor with gifts and lunches and are still denied." Richard made a face. "It's shameless really."

"Gifts like a box of chocolates?" Reese asked.

Richard raised an eyebrow at him. "Touché, Detective."

"But this is great," I said. "Now we have a whole list of people who had just as much of a motive to kill Marcie as Richard. Maybe more if they'd been trying to get on the list for years. Killing someone is a desperate act, not the act of someone who merely got miffed. We should be looking for someone who'd reached the end of their tether with Marcie. Someone desperate."

"We?" Reese leveled his gaze at me.

"I mean you," I said, trying out Kate's method of eyelash fluttering. "Of course you. I'm a wedding planner, not a cop."

"Do you have something in your eye, darling?" Richard asked.

Reese grinned as I stopped batting my lashes. "Oh, how I wish you actually believed that."

"I do know you're going to need our help to figure out the most likely suspects." I took a bite of my pasta, feeling better I could do something to help clear Richard, especially since I'd been the one to suggest he give Marcie a box of chocolates. Before my boyfriend could give me his usual warning, I continued. "But aside from that, I promise not to meddle in your case."

Richard stood and picked up Reese's empty plate. "But really, Detective, don't you think calling the victim my arch enemy is a bit dramatic?"

"Leave the dramatics to the professionals," I whispered once Richard was out of earshot.

❧ 7 ❧

"So Reese thinks it was one of the other people who were kicked off the list who tried to kill Marcie?" Kate asked, stepping out of the passenger side of my CRV once I'd pulled to a stop in front of the Intercontinental Hotel at The Wharf. Since it was not quite ten in the morning, the area had not yet come alive, although I knew the waterfront restaurants and shops on the boardwalk would get busy by midday.

I opened my car door and handed my keys to the valet attendant. "We have a walk-through with a bride and the catering director," I told him and joined Kate on the other side of the car, barely glancing at the docked sailboats at the pier. Even though The Wharf DC, as we called it, was one of the newer luxury hotels built at the now-upscale Washington Harbor, I'd been to enough meetings and walk-throughs for Amelia's wedding that I felt like it had been there forever.

"I'm not sure if Reese thinks that yet," I said, walking through the glass doors one of the doormen held open for us, "but I tried to nudge him in that direction last night over dinner."

We crossed the high-ceilinged, ivory-marble lobby and headed for the double staircases leading up to the ballroom level. As we walked up the stairs, our shoes tapping with each step and the chunky heel of Kate's knee-high black boots adding an additional loud slap, I glanced at the oversized pendant lights dangling at different heights above our heads. The hotel used lots of gold in the decor, so it felt modern without being stark.

"Isn't that called tampering with a police investigation," Kate asked, "and haven't you gotten in trouble for that before?"

"Suggesting other suspects is hardly tampering." We reached the top of the stairs, and I headed for the ballroom. "Anyway, we know Richard didn't have anything to do with Marcus's death."

"Do we?" Kate hurried along behind me. "He seemed pretty livid with the guy the one time we saw them together."

"It's Richard," I reminded her, stopping in front of the ballroom doors so she could catch up. "He threatens murder if he sees someone with a poorly knotted Windsor."

"Good point." Kate tugged the jacket of her snug-fitting black suit. "And I can't see him wanting to kill Marcie if he was attempting to get in her good graces."

I opened the large door and peeked my head inside the room. Empty. "We're the first ones here." I held the door for Kate and stepped inside. The ballroom had tall ceilings and equally tall windows taking up two walls overlooking the waterfront and the Potomac River. Since most hotel ballrooms were relegated to the basement, the natural light and breathtaking views made this one of my favorite new venues in the city. Plus, it faced west and got beautiful sunsets.

"Remind me again, who's coming to this walk-through?" Kate asked. "And while you're doing that, remind me why we're having another walk-through only days before the wedding."

"Since the final guest count is due to the hotel today, Amelia wanted to give it in person."

"What kind of bride wants to give the final guest count in person?" Kate shook her head. "That's an over the phone or quick email type of thing."

I dropped my voice so it wouldn't echo in the large empty

room. "The same kind of bride who makes her flower girls wear cupid wings and her ring bearers carry bows and arrows."

Kate shuddered. "I do not look forward to wrangling children who are armed."

"I can't imagine the arrows are real," I said, hoping very much I was right and the wedding wouldn't include multiple lacerations.

"So we aren't the first ones." Buster's deep voice made me turn toward the door as he and his business partner, Mack, joined us.

"What are you two doing here?" Kate asked. "I know you don't allow changes to the floral order this close in."

Our favorite floral designers were strict about two things. One, final floral orders had to be in ten days before the event and two, no cursing in front of them. The first rule was practical and the second was because they were members of a born-again Christian biker gang.

The chains on Buster's black leather pants jingled as he walked, and his bulk blocked my view of his almost equally sizable partner, Mack, no doubt also decked out in their customary head-to-toe leather.

"Amelia wanted to discuss how the giant X and O tables will be arranged throughout the room. We figured it would be easier to have her show us than to rely on a diagram. You know we have to have the floor plan exact since the centerpieces for the O tables hang from the ceiling." Buster stroked his dark goatee as he looked up. "It's a shame she wants to add so much frill. The room is beautiful as it is."

I held up a finger. "But it's not pink and red."

"It will be on Saturday," Mack said in a singsong voice, stepping out from behind Buster and revealing a black front-facing baby carrier complete with a front-facing baby.

"Merry!" Kate clapped her hands when she saw the baby girl smiling and waving her fat fists. "She's gotten so big since the last time I saw her."

Mack pivoted to face me, and Merry swung along with him. "I know what you're thinking, Annabelle, and I know it's not professional to bring a baby to a meeting with a bride, but her mother is in class, and we didn't have anyone else to leave her with."

I took one of Merry's little feet and jiggled it. "You know I don't care one way or the other, but brides aren't excited to share the spotlight with anything cuter than them."

"That's what I said." Buster gave his partner a look. "If Amelia thinks we're anything less than 100 percent focused on her and her wedding, she might have a breakdown."

"Or worse," Kate said. "Write you a bad review."

"Can Buster handle the meeting?" I asked. "It's not like you both need to be here, do you?"

Mack raised an eyebrow.

"Never mind. Of course Amelia will ask where you are." I sized up the baby in her pink hat with tiny bear ears as she gave me a toothless grin. "Any chance you can flip the carrier around to your back and have her face the wall the entire time?"

"You don't think the bride will notice a giggling lump on Mack's back?" Kate asked. "I doubt we can get Amelia that drunk *that* fast."

Mack snapped his fingers. "I've got it. We'll switch off holding Merry. One person will stay in another room with her and after a few minutes, someone will tag them out."

"So there will always be three people in the meeting but never all of us at the same time?" Buster asked.

"I feel like this never works on sitcoms," I said.

"It's worth a try." Mack bounced the baby in front of him. "I'll duck out with her. Annabelle, you tag me out once the meeting gets started, and I'll run in and apologize for being late."

He hurried toward the ballroom doors and slipped out before I could argue.

Buster wiped a hand across his bald head. "Just the idea of being deceitful is making me sweat. The Bible says 'No one who practices deceit will dwell in my house.'"

"It's not deceit," Kate said. "It's more of an omission. Mack *will* be sorry to be late. By the time it's my turn, I'm sure I'll legitimately need to go to the ladies' room. As long as no one lies outright, we shouldn't have any house dwelling issues."

"Why am I the first one tagging him out?" My palms felt sweaty. "I'm not sure this is such a good idea."

"Did someone have a new idea about my wedding?" Amelia's high-pitched voice reverberated through the room and made us all jump.

"There's our bride!" Kate matched Amelia's excited voice as she rushed over to greet the petite blonde in heels almost as high as my assistant's.

After we exchanged greetings, Amelia scanned our group then stuck out her bottom lip. "Where's Mack?"

"He'll be here," I said, and Buster looked like he might faint.

Kate looped her arm through the bride's. "The hotel's catering director hasn't come down yet, but we can get started with the floral decor."

"Without Mack?"

"Why don't I see if he's in the lobby? He may not know we're already in the ballroom," I said. "I need to pop into the ladies' room anyway."

I took quick steps out of the room. Where was Mack hiding? I poked my head into the nearest meeting room and breathed a sigh of relief. "There you are. Amelia's asking about you."

Mack lifted Merry from the carrier and unhooked it from his waist, handing the baby to me and holding out the carrier. I shook my head. "By the time I get that contraption figured out, it'll be my turn to go back inside." I put the baby across one shoulder, and she took hold of my ponytail.

"I'll be back before you know it." Mack gave baby Merry a final worried glance and lumbered out of the room.

I walked a long path down the length of the room, rubbing Merry's back as I did. Luckily, she was too entertained trying to chew my hair to be upset Mack had gone. My phone trilled in my purse, and I dug it out with one hand.

"Richard," I said after I saw his name pop up onto my screen. "I can't really talk--"

"I'm at the police station," Richard's voice came out in short bursts. "They brought me in for more questioning. It wasn't even Reese who picked me up. It was a chubby fellow."

"Hobbes?" I said. "That's Reese's sometimes partner. Alexandra brought him to our holiday party."

I hoped Richard wouldn't want to go into the odd pairing of our glamorous cake baker and the doughy detective, because I had no explanations. Merry gurgled, and I jiggled her while I paced.

"What was that?" Richard asked. "A laugh?"

"Of course not." I didn't know how to explain the bizarre switcheroo scenario I'd gotten myself involved in without it sounding as ridiculous as it was. "Why are they questioning you again? Reese doesn't think you have a motive."

"That was before they talked to the folks down at Fleurir."

"The place where you got the chocolates?"

My hair slipped from the baby's grasp and she began fussing. I held the phone to my ear with my head pressed against one shoulder as I tried to quiet her.

"Really, Annabelle." Richard let out his breath in a huff. "Why are you crying? I'm the one about to be interrogated."

"I'm not. I'm . . . Never mind. What could the people at Fleurir have said that would make the police think you're guilty?"

Richard's voice became a whisper. "Apparently they heard me talking to you on the phone when I was there picking up the order. When you told me I should give a box to Marcie, and I was hemming and hawing over it."

"I remember," I said. "Why would that be a problem?"

"Do you also remember when I told you I'd rather give the editor of *Capital Weddings* a dose of hemlock than a box of chocolates?"

I cringed as baby drool dribbled onto my shoulder and was glad the jacket of my dark-brown suit was wool and not silk. I thought back to the conversation. Although it was hard to isolate the dramatic things Richard said on a daily basis, the word 'hemlock' did ring a bell. Merry emitted a high-pitched wail.

"Exactly how I feel, darling," Richard said, sniffling. "I can't tell you how nice it is to get some real empathy instead of your usual level-headed advice."

I handed the baby the phone so she and Richard could cry together.

❧ 8 ❧

"I'm all for meeting the boys for lunch," Kate said, "but after that meeting with Amelia, I think I need a drink."

I turned my car down one of side streets near the Washington Cathedral and searched for parking. "Cafe Deluxe has a bar, although I was hoping we could get some work done this afternoon."

Kate pointed to a space between a minivan and an SUV. "I do need to work on my Valentine's Day plans. Good thing Fern is joining us."

Developing a spreadsheet to handle her multiple dates wasn't exactly the kind of work I'd meant, but I focused on backing my car into the tight space without tapping the other car' bumpers.

"Richard was lucky Fern's salon isn't far and he had a gap in his appointments." Kate flipped down the mirror in the passenger side visor and inspected her lipstick. "If he'd had to wait for us to pick him up from the police station after our meeting all the way across town, he would not have been pleased."

I doubted he was pleased as it was. I locked my car with a click of my key fob, and Kate and I walked across the street and down the sidewalk to the restaurant. A quick glance at the art deco neon sign above the entrance told me we were at the right place, although since it was winter, the tables with their red umbrellas did not crowd the patio like usual. Once we'd pushed through the glass doors, we were enveloped by both the warmth and the savory scent of food. I scanned the room and the white-clothed tables, finally spotting Fern's arm waving high from the far side of the restaurant.

"We got a spot away from the action," he said once we'd weaved our way through the sea of square tables to a booth along the wall, "so we could confer in private."

I noticed Fern wore a salmon-colored suit with a white shirt underneath, the collar spread at his neck. "Already in the spirit of the holiday?"

He flicked a hand at his outfit and the enormous topaz ring on his finger nearly blinded me when it caught the light. "This is just a warm-up, sweetie."

Kate slipped into the booth next to him. "Is that the Pantone color of the year?"

Fern smiled as he adjusted his French cuffs. "Living Coral? Why yes it is, and aren't you sweet to notice?" He took in Kate's black suit and my dark-brown one. "At least someone is adding a pop of color to this crew."

I took the seat next to Richard, who was slumped over a martini. So much for discouraging day drinking. "I take it things didn't go well with the police?"

Richard glanced at me and then at the cocktail as if seeing it for the first time. "I didn't order this."

Fern giggled and pulled it toward him. "He's holding my backup."

"Your backup?" I asked.

"You know," Kate said. "When the bar's backed up, you order two drinks so you don't have to wait forever for your second one."

Clearly, I was not well versed in bar strategy. I eyed Fern as he took a sip from the wide-rimmed glass. "So that's your second drink of the day before noon?"

"It's been a trying day so far," he said. "First I had to fix a botched dye job. Then I had to make Myrna Thomas look like she has hair, which is like trying to spread cotton candy across a bowling ball, and then I spent almost an entire hour at the police station."

Richard crossed his arms in front of him. "It took an hour at the station because you insisted on doing the officers' colors."

Fern took another sip. "What could I do? They were all wearing a lifeless shade of navy blue, which everyone knows is not nearly as versatile as black."

"It was their uniform," Richard said.

"That doesn't mean it can't be stylish." Fern drained his glass and circled his hand overhead to summon another. "They could at least use a fabric with a pattern. Maybe a nice ombre where the blue tones shift from baby blue to a darker blue."

Richard twisted to face me. "Next time, just send a firing squad."

"Our day hasn't been a picnic either," Kate said, motioning for the waiter to bring her the same drink as Fern. "We had another meeting with the bride for Saturday, and we had to hide Merry from her the entire time."

"Merry?" Fern blinked hard. "The baby came to your meeting? How did she get there?"

After the next cocktail, I was cutting him off. "Buster and Mack brought her since Prue was in class."

"Didn't I tell you this baby thing wouldn't be smooth sailing?" Richard said. "It's only a matter of time before she's coming to wedding setups and motorcycle ride alongs."

Bold words from a man who carried his dog in his man bag and had been know to bring the tiny canine to walk-throughs and wedding setups.

"The bride never knew she was there," Kate said. "We took turns ducking out of the meeting and entertaining her. Amelia probably thinks we all have intestinal issues, but she doesn't suspect we were hiding a baby."

Richard snapped his head around. "Wait a second. When you were lamenting with me over the phone, was that you or the baby?"

I felt my cheeks flush and stared intently at the menu. "I should probably get a salad, although the chicken pot pie looks delicious."

Richard sucked in his breath. "Oh. My. G . . . I was on the phone with a baby?"

"I'll bet the conversation with her was better than my conversation with Mitzy Winkler this morning." Fern plucked a martini off the waiter's tray before the man could set it on the table. "Talking to that woman is like talking to a tree stump but less interesting."

Richard and I ordered drinks--nonalcoholic ones--and I shooed the waiter away before Fern could remember to order another backup cocktail.

"The important thing is what the police think," I said. "They can't believe you were serious about that offhand remark over the phone. People say they'd like to kill other people all the time."

"I know I do," Fern muttered over his martini.

"Luckily, your boyfriend isn't as eager to pin the crime on me as his portly partner is. Once I explained everything to Reese, he told me I was free to go."

"Did he mention anything about the suspects you gave him to check out?" I asked.

"Dad Bod Detective didn't seem focused on anyone but me."

"Hobbes," I reminded him. I wished Reese's sometime partner wasn't so closely involved. He didn't understand Richard or the wedding industry. My boyfriend, however, was familiar enough with Richard's flair for the dramatic to know that him threatening to poison someone with hemlock was just another day at the office.

"I don't like that they haven't moved on from you as a suspect." I tapped my fingers against the table. "They must not have come up with any other credible options. What we need to do is make a list of all the people who could have wanted Marcie out of the way. Not just vendors who didn't get on the list."

Kate took a drink from her martini. "Isn't this the kind of thing Reese hates you to do?"

"He hates for me to interfere in his investigations," I said, waving a hand to encompass our table. "This is a few friends discussing potential murder suspects over a work lunch."

"Sounds like sticks in one, half dozen in the other," Kate said.

Fern bobbed his head up and down. "Exactly."

I ignored Kate's mangled expression. "Richard and I already determined there were more vendors than him upset about the list. The band agent Ron Tinker, Petals and Petunias, and Skyfall Video all got kicked off the list this year."

Fern's eyes widened then his face went blank. "Never heard of them."

"Probably why they were removed from the list." I avoided Richard's eyes. "Not everything about the list is political."

"I know Ron Tinker," Richard said. "He's got a temper almost as outsized as his ego."

Kate snapped her fingers. "Is he that pushy guy who mails us all his press clippings?"

"I just throw away anything from his company's return address," I said. "He probably annoyed so many people no one voted for him. But if he has a bad temper, maybe he's the one who wanted to kill Marcie. He probably blamed her for taking him off the list, even though I'm sure he alienated everyone else in our industry as much as he did us."

"It's still a bit of a leap from being angry you're off the list to murdering someone," Kate said. "It's not like killing Marcie would have guaranteed they'd get back on the list."

Fern nudged her, and his drink almost sloshed out of his glass. "I don't think killers are your most reasonable people, sweetie."

"Kate's right." I took a drink from the iced tea the waiter set down in front of me before reaching for the sugar caddy. "We need to widen our net. Who else might have hated Marcie enough to kill her?"

Richard shrugged. "Who really knows her? Until we dropped by her office in December, I'd never laid eyes on her."

"She hasn't been with the magazine long," I said, "and I'm not sure where she worked before that. I do know it wasn't in weddings. Not in DC at least. Who would know more about her?"

"One of the girls in my assistant happy hour crew interns at *Capital Weddings*." Kate pulled out her phone and began scrolling down the screen. "I can ask her."

"That's a good start," I said. "Maybe I can ask around and see if any of our planner friends knew her better than we did."

Fern leaned back in the booth and slid down and sideways a few inches. "What we really need is to find out who does her hair. Then we'd know everything we need to know. What kind of cut does she have?"

"Long," I said, trying to remember more about the editor's hairstyle.

"Blunt cut," Kate said, not looking up from her phone. "No color or tapered sides. A few split ends."

Fern drummed two fingers against his bottom lip. "Doubtful it was done by any of the premier stylists." He dropped his voice and glanced over his shoulder. "She might have used someone in the suburbs."

"I hope we're not pinning my entire get out of jail strategy on his Hair Mousse Mafia connection," Richard said.

Kate clinked her empty glass with Fern's. "There are worse ways to solve a crime."

Richard sunk down next to me. "I'm doomed."

9

"I'm telling you, I don't need a haircut," I said as Fern propelled me through the doors of his tony Georgetown salon.

The long, narrow space was both simple and ornate with huge gilded mirrors hanging in front of the two stylists' red chairs and carved wooden credenzas used to hold brushes, combs, and styling product. The dark hardwood floors gleamed, Kate's footsteps echoing off them as she walked ahead of us.

"Do you remember what you were wearing the last time Fern gave you a cut?" she asked, sinking into one of the chairs and spinning around in it.

"What?" I asked. "How would I remember that? It was probably six months ago."

"I rest my case."

Fern patted the other chair and swiveled it around so I could sit down. "Sweetie, if I have to go another day looking at those raggedy ends, I think I'm going to cry."

"Fine," I said, dropping my purse onto the floor next to the nearest credenza, "but I really don't have time for this. Not only do we have a wedding coming up, but Richard's a suspect in a murder case and it's kind of my fault. Plus, it's Valentine's Day on Sunday, and I have no idea what to get my boyfriend."

Fern unfurled a black smock over my head and fastened it at the back of my neck. "That is a lot, but that's why it's so good you're here." He winked at my reflection in the mirror. "I'm an expert at solving problems."

From my experience, Fern usually created more dramatic problems, but maybe it was different when he was on his turf. And this luxe salon with its smell of high-end beauty products and the sound of soft classical Muzak playing overhead was definitely his domain.

Fern bent over the credenza, opening the door underneath and producing a bottle of champagne. "Bubbles, ladies?"

I peered down. "Do you have a mini fridge in there?"

He put a finger to his lips. "I just give this to my special clients or the ones I want to get drunk so they'll shut up."

I hoped I wasn't one of the latter. "Just a smidge," I said as he filled my flute to the rim, then filled his own and Kate's just as high.

Fern tossed back the contents of his glass and turned to my hair. He pulled out the black elastic and fanned my reddish-brown hair across my shoulders. I was surprised it had gotten so long, although I didn't know why since I hadn't touched it in months. I got so busy I forgot personal things like haircuts and manicures. It was why I wore my hair long and my nails short.

"I say we lose a few inches, give it shape, and add face-framing layers," Fern said, eyeing my barely touched glass. "I don't suppose you've had enough champagne to let me do bangs?"

"Not even close," I said. "And no color."

Fern frowned. "You break my heart, Annabelle, but fine. I'll cut it dry before we wash it." He reached for a shiny pair of gold scissors. "Now that we've decided that, let's discuss the important issue at hand."

I nodded. "Richard being a murder suspect?"

Fern gave a snort of laughter. "That's happened before, sweetie.

What hasn't happened before is you having a live-in love on Valentine's Day." He tilted my head down as he brushed my hair over my eyes.

Kate used one foot to stop her chair next to me from spinning. "Now we're talking. I originally thought sexy lingerie, but I don't think she can pull it off. Not with a straight face at least."

"Surprising him with a dominatrix catsuit is out?" Fern asked.

"That was always out," Kate said. "Annabelle can't pull off leather."

"You know I can hear you, right?" I tried to peer through the curtain of hair, but Fern tilted my head down. "What ever happened to sweet and romantic? Like a card and maybe some cologne?"

I couldn't see Fern's reaction, but I could hear him pretending to snore. "Fine, aside from kinky stuff, what would you recommend?"

"You could bake him something," Kate said.

"We don't want to ruin his flat stomach." Fern snipped as he talked. "Too many men get married or move in with someone and get fat. I, for one, enjoy his physique and do not want you to ruin it. No baked goods."

"That doesn't leave us with much," Kate said. "Especially since we don't know what he has planned for her."

Fern brushed my hair back so I could see again. "Maybe he's planning an evening of S & M for you."

"I seriously doubt it," I said, finally taking a sip of champagne and feeling the bubbles tickle my nose as I swallowed. "Aside from having handcuffs, I don't think he's into that stuff."

Fern's eyes grew wide. "I forgot he had handcuffs." He put down his scissors and used both hands to fan himself. "I might need a moment."

I shook out my smock and significant chunks of hair fell to the floor. "Maybe we should stop talking about Reese and move on to figuring out how to help Richard. All this talk of Valentine's Day is stressing me out and overheating Fern."

Kate grinned as she watched Fern lean against the back of my chair. "Maybe you're right."

"The key is finding out who had a motive to kill Marcie since she was clearly the intended target," I said, assessing my slightly shorter hair in the mirror as Fern composed himself by swigging another glass of champagne. "The problem is we don't know enough about her to know if she had enemies."

Fern took a black Bluetooth device and hooked it to his ear. "Didn't I tell you I could find out anything through my hairdresser network?" He picked up his comb again and started to brush my hair straight down my back. "Siri, call Rudolpho."

I caught Kate's eyes and she raised her hands and shrugged, which meant she had no clue who this Rudolpho was either. Even though Fern worked with us on nearly every wedding, his salon business was his bread and butter, and I knew he was as well known in the world of stylists as he was in the world of weddings. I suspected Fern did wedding hair with us as a diversion from his daily cut-and-color routine for the wealthy women of DC.

Fern eyed the back of my hair before combing a section high above my head and shearing off the ends. "Rudolpho, sweetie, it's Fern." He paused and let out a laugh. "Well, aren't you a doll?" Another pause. "Oh, go on."

Kate cocked an eyebrow at me as she plucked a brush from the credenza in front of her chair and began rolling the ends of her bob around the round bristles. I'd always been envious her hair held curl and shape even after twelve-hour wedding days, while my straight hair lost any bounce within the first ten minutes. Hence my habit of wearing it in a bun during weddings. It drove Fern crazy that I rarely styled my hair, but buns or pony-tails kept it out of my face and made it one less thing I had to worry about.

"You know I would love that," Fern said as he walked around me, appraising my cut. "Quickie question before I run, you don't happen to know who does the editor of *Capital Weddings*, do you? The tall girl with long dark hair. Blunt cut."

"What about sexy underwear?" Kate whispered to me as she replaced the brush.

"Didn't we decide sexy lingerie was too much?" I asked.

Kate waved a hand at me. "Not for you. For him. What about getting Reese some red boxer briefs? He does wear boxer briefs, doesn't he?"

"Yes, but. . . " I stopped once I realized I'd revealed what kind of underwear my boyfriend wore. "I don't think he'd wear red underwear."

"Too bad," Fern said, and it took me a moment to realize he was still speaking to Rudolpho. "Do you think Jacques would know?"

"You never know until you try. It's not like I'm suggesting you get him a thong made to look like an elephant's trunk." She winked at me. "Not for your first Valentine's Day at least."

The thought of Reese wearing an elephant thong made my cheeks flush, and I was glad Fern was too occupied with his call to have heard or noticed.

"Kisses to you too," Fern said, looking up. "Well, we know it wasn't Rudolpho or any of the stylists in his salons, but he thinks Jacques might know."

"Too bad you don't keep a central database of clients," I said. "That way you could track them when they switch stylists and know which ones are the nightmares."

Fern tapped his comb on my shoulder. "Not a bad idea, sweetie."

"We should do that with brides," Kate said.

I flicked more hair off my smock. "Except by the time we know they're nightmares, they're already married."

"What do we think?" Fern leaned down so his head was even with mine and studied me in the mirror. "Safe enough for you?"

He'd trimmed a couple of inches off the ends and tapered the sides, parting my hair on the left as usual. I had to admit it looked a lot better. "It's perfect. Thank you."

"Of course it is." Fern straightened. "I'll clean it up after it's wet. Let me get the water warmed for you, then I'll take you back to wash." He headed to the back of the salon as he asked Siri to call Jacques.

"This hairdresser angle may not pan out," I said to Kate. "And even if it does, Marcie might not be the type to tell her stylist her life history."

Kate shrugged. "Maybe not. You don't think Reese would be willing to do a background search on her and share his findings, do you?"

I stifled a laugh. "Definitely not. I'm sure he's doing background on her, but I doubt he thought of the hairdresser connection. He'd be less than thrilled we've roped Fern into asking other stylists about her."

Kate spun her chair to face me. "See? This is why we end up investigating. The cops don't approach things from the creative angles we do."

"I doubt Reese sees it that way."

Fern hurried toward us holding a short stack of brown towels. "I got a hit, girls. Marcie gets her hair done at Jacques's salon. She couldn't get in with Jacques himself, of course, but she goes to one of his second-tier stylists."

Kate stood up. "Great. What did the second-tier stylist say about her?"

Fern shook a finger then pointed to his earpiece. "Mmm hmm. She said that?" He raised an eyebrow. "I owe you one." A giggle. "You know I would. Mmm hmm. Don't be a stranger."

"Well?" Kate said when he'd clearly hung up.

Fern dropped the towels in her arms and pulled me up by the elbow. "According to Marcie's stylist, she got the same cut every time and hasn't made any significant hair changes recently." He shifted his eyes to me. "Kind of like some people I know."

We headed to the shiny washbasins lined up against the back wall behind a partition, and Fern plunked me down in the nearest chair. "A switch in hairstyle can signal a major life change," he continued, "but Marcie hasn't done anything like that."

He took one of the towels from Kate and folded it around my neck then pushed me down so my hair fell into the attached basin.

I sighed as I tried to get in a comfortable position with my neck angled back. "So another dead end?"

"Not exactly." Fern pulled the nozzle out and let the water run over his hand for a second. "She may not have changed her hair, but her stylist said she'd been jumpy the last time she'd been in. Almost like she was afraid of something."

Kate put a hand to her mouth and dropped the remaining towel. "Do you think she suspected her life was in danger?"

Fern turned the spray on my hair and the warm water spilled down my head, blocking out all sounds but the rushing water. I closed my eyes and thought about what Fern had discovered. If Marcie knew her life might be in danger, I wondered what else she knew and wasn't telling.

❧ 10 ❧

"I'm glad we're not going back to the office right away," Kate said, "although it's a shame not to take your new hair out for a spin someplace fun."

I flipped my blown-out hair off my shoulder as I turned onto P Street, trying to fight the urge to put it up in a ponytail. "It's not a new sports car. Since we know Marcie was afraid of something, we should try to find out what that was. It might be the key to the entire case and clearing Richard as a suspect."

"Unless she was afraid of Richard," Kate said. "That's always a possibility."

"She didn't know him enough to be scared. You have to really know Richard to be properly terrified."

"You make a good point." She leaned forward and drummed her polished pink nails on the black boots skimming her knees. "Don't you think popping into the *Capital Weddings* offices is exactly what your boyfriend would call meddling?"

"What he calls meddling, I call being a supportive colleague." I cast a quick glance over my shoulder as I merged into the traffic heading downtown. "And I have every intention of telling him what we've found out about Marcie. Is it my fault he didn't answer his cell phone just now?"

"Now that's a conversation I'd like to be a fly on the wall for."

I gnawed the edge of my lip. She was right. Reese would be less than thrilled to discover Fern had been calling fellow hairdressers to get the scoop on the intended murder victim. Even if it did result in a potential clue. Forget Valentine's Day. I was going to need to whip out the gifts and candy just to make up to him after the murder investigation.

"Let's look at this as marketing strategy," I said. "It's always a good idea for us to be in tight with *Capital Weddings*, right? And what better way to ingratiate ourselves with them than to stop by and offer condolences?"

"I can think of a lot of things I'd want more than condolences," Kate muttered, "but I see where you're going with this."

I turned onto I Street and snagged a street parking space from a car as it was pulling away from the curb. Plugging the space number into the mobile parking app on my phone, I paid for an hour in advance and hoped I wouldn't need more.

Kate pulled her coat tight around her neck and glanced up at the steel-and-glass building housing *Capital Weddings*. "The last time we came here, things didn't end so well."

"The last time we had Richard, and he was whipped up before we arrived. This time will be different."

"I hope so." Kate teetered beside me in her boots. "I'd hate for the people at the magazine to associate high-pitched shrieking and death threats with us."

We hurried out of the cold and into the warmth of the building lobby. Aside from an expanse of white marble floor and elevators, the space held nothing but a front desk and drowsy security guard who barely looked up when we signed in. We were quiet on the quick elevator ride up. I know I felt a bit nervous to be visiting the crime scene, although the lobby had betrayed no clue there had been a murder in the building.

The small waiting area for the magazine was empty and we

paused at reception. An arrangement of white lilies sat to one side of the desk, and the pungent perfume of the flowers mixed with the smell of coffee made my stomach turn.

"I don't see any crime scene tape or cops, but the place seems dead," Kate said, then cringed. "I didn't mean it that way."

"You're right." I peeked my head out of the reception area to the open floor plan room dotted with cubicles. "It looks like half the staff called in sick."

Kate craned her neck around me. "I wonder where it happened. The murder, I mean. Do you know where Marcus's desk was?"

"Close to Marcie's office, I assume, since he was her assistant." I let my eyes wander to the editor's office at the far side of the space and overlooking the street. The door was closed. Either she was holed away inside or had decided not to come in. Neither would have surprised me.

A curvy redhead approached us. "Can I help you?"

I put on my best sincerely fake smile. "I'm Annabelle Archer with Wedding Belles and this is my associate Kate. We're friends with Marcie and wanted to see how she's doing."

This seemed to appease the redhead because the wrinkle between her eyes relaxed. "How nice of you. It's been just awful around here since . . ."

Kate put a hand on her arm. "Isn't it tragic about Marcus?"

"Did you know him?" the woman asked, digging a crumpled tissue from her pants pocket.

Kate nodded but didn't speak.

The woman dabbed the tissue to her nose. "I still can't believe it. It could have been any one of us. We all tried the chocolates."

Again, I was struck by how odd it was to poison one chocolate truffle out of an entire box. The killer either assumed the victim would eat the entire box or knew the one flavor they'd go for.

"And you are. . .?" Kate prodded.

"Sorry." The woman swiped at her eyes and held out a hand. "Cassandra. I'm one of the assistant editors."

"I think I recognize your name from some of the articles," I said, trying to make a connection. "Didn't you do the feature on edible favors?"

She smiled through her tears and nodded.

"It was really good," I said before switching gears. "Do you remember Marcie trying any of the truffles before she gave them away?"

The woman thought for a moment. "I don't think so, but she might have when she walked through the main office. She didn't so much give them to Marcus as give them to him to share with the team."

"That was nice of her," Kate said. "Marcie must be a great boss to work for."

Cassandra bobbed her head up and down. "She's the best. How many other bosses would share their gifts with their coworkers?"

"So no one here has a problem with her?" I asked, trying to keep my voice light.

"With Marcie?" She stopped wiping her nose. "Of course not. Everyone loves working for her. I can tell you she's tons better than the last editor."

I barely remembered the name of the last editor because she'd come and gone so quickly, and I was pretty sure I'd never met her. Marcie had already earned a reputation for being more involved with the wedding community and more friendly than her predecessor.

"And Marcus liked her?" Kate asked, rubbing her hand up and down the woman's arm.

"Oh, yeah. She and Marcus were tight. I think he spent more time in her office than at his own desk. She's pretty devastated about what happened. She's barely left her office all day."

I glanced at the closed door. "It must be scary to know the chocolates meant for you were poisoned."

Cassandra shook her head sharply. "It must have been a mistake of some kind, because I can't think of anyone who'd want to kill Marcie."

"I know she's upset now, but do you think she's seemed nervous lately?" I asked.

"Nervous?"

"You know." I dropped my voice as I noticed a couple of heads poke out from their cubbies. "Jumpy or scared about something. Anxious perhaps?"

"Well, she hates getting calls from irritated vendors, and she definitely got a few of those after the list came out at the end of December. This year she even got a bouquet of dead, black roses from someone."

Kate made a face. "Creepy. Do you know who sent them?"

"I doubt the person signed the card," I mumbled, wondering what kind of psycho had decided that was appropriate. Even Richard, who'd been pretty steamed about being taken off the list, would never have stooped to sending dead roses. Primarily because he would never send a gift that wasn't visually appealing, no matter how upset he was. The dead flowers could have been what had spooked Marcie and what her stylist had picked up on. It would make sense. Black, rotting bouquets weren't a feel-good type of gift.

"You're right. No one took credit for the dead roses," Cassandra said. "It shook Marcie up, but other than that I wouldn't say she's been jumpy. She wasn't thrilled the lock on her office had been broken, but she didn't think it had anything to do with the upset wedding vendors."

"Her office was broken into?" I asked.

"Actually, no," Cassandra said. "The lock was damaged so she couldn't lock the door, but no one broke in. She thought the cleaning crew did it accidentally or something."

I tapped my foot against the carpet. "When did this happen?"

"The day before yesterday. Marcie noticed it at lunch when she tried to lock her office as she left."

I did a mental calculation. That would have been the day Richard dropped off the chocolates. It seemed awfully coincidental that the lock on Marcie's office was damaged. It also meant the chocolates had been in the unlocked room overnight before she gave them to her assistant to pass around. Without a lock on the door, the killer would have had access at any time Marcie was out to tamper with the truffles.

"I wish we knew who sent those black flowers," I said more to myself than anyone. "And who broke the lock on her office door."

"So do I," Marcie said from behind me.

I put a hand to my heart as I turned around. The editor's eyes were red rimmed and held an expression I couldn't place. When had she come out of her office, and how much of our questioning had she heard?

"**J**ust the person we came here to see," Kate said, recovering more quickly than I did and pulling Marcie in for a hug.

Marcie didn't return Kate's embrace, and her expression remained wooden. I wondered if she was in shock or if she considered us the enemy since we were friends with Richard.

"They came by to see how you were doing," Cassandra explained, her own expression more guarded now that her boss had joined us. "They said they were your friends."

"We hope we aren't imposing," I said. "We were worried about you after yesterday and wanted to see if there was anything we could do."

"We have some experience with dealing with murders in the workplace," Kate said.

I tried not to slap my hand on my forehead. The last thing I wanted Marcie to know was how many crime investigations we'd been involved with. It did not make us, or Richard, look good to know how many dead bodies had turned up at our weddings.

Cassandra blinked hard a few times then let out a nervous

laugh, and Kate and I joined her. Better she think Kate was making an odd joke, I thought.

"I came by to try to get some work done," Marcie said, not joining in on the laughing. "I thought it would be better than staying at home, but it's not."

"We're so sorry about your assistant," I said. "I know it must have been an awful shock."

She bit her thumbnail. "Everything was fine when I left the office yesterday morning. I gave Marcus the box of chocolates to share with the team then ran out to make it to Love Brunch on time. I never saw him again."

"You didn't like chocolate truffles?" I asked, trying to make my question sound as conversational as possible.

Marcie dropped her chipped thumbnail from her mouth. "Normally I'm a pretty serious chocoholic, but I'd decided to drop a few post-holiday pounds."

I gave the editor a quick once-over. She was pretty trim, but that didn't mean anything since Fern regularly went on crash diets and never needed to. Even Kate did the occasional carb fast, and she'd been a size four since the day I met her.

"Did anyone know you were dieting?" I asked.

She twitched one shoulder up and down. "I told Marcus, but that was about it." Her voice broke. "I told him everything."

So no one but her assistant knew Marcie had sworn off sweets. That meant the killer assumed she'd at least try them since she was a self-proclaimed chocoholic. But how could he have known she'd eat the one poisoned truffle?

"Did you have a favorite type of chocolate?" I asked, then realized it sounded like I was interrogating her. I tried to soften my question. "I love the caramels, but hate the ones with nuts."

"And I love anything with nuts," Kate said.

"Me too," Cassandra said, reminding me she was still standing with us. "But the chocolates in the box Marcus had were all really unique flavors."

That sounded like Richard. He would have picked the most

exotic chocolates. Now I remembered Marcie mentioning the interesting varieties.

Marcie nibbled her nail again. "I read the flavors but was afraid if I tried one, I'd eat them all. The box sat on my desk untouched from the time it was dropped off until I gave it to Marcus."

Meaning it would have been nearly impossible to add poison to the box after it was delivered unless someone came in after hours. Not good news for Richard.

"There was a card explaining each flavor," Cassandra said. "I got the lavender almond. I remember Marcus tried the one in the middle. It was the biggest, and I think it was cherry liquor. He said the booze had a kick."

I didn't point out that the kick he tasted was most likely the poison and not the booze.

Marcie drew in a sharp breath. "He ate the cherry one?"

Cassandra nodded. "He took first pick and said he loved cherries."

"That's my favorite too," Marcie said, her voice barely a whisper. "Marcus and I both loved cherry cordials. It was a joke between us. We gave each other cheap drugstore boxes of chocolate covered cherries at Christmas for years."

"Who else knew this about you?" I asked.

"It wasn't a secret," she said. "We did it last year, and I'm pretty sure we kept the boxes on our desks this year."

Her colleague snapped her fingers "That's right. I remember Marcus eating those around the holidays. He gave me a few."

Marcie smiled for the first time. "They were pretty cheap to buy. It was a joke between us. We started exchanging them back when we couldn't afford better gifts and then kept doing it even when we could buy the fancier stuff."

Kate tilted her head at Marcie. "I thought Marcus was relatively new at *Capital Weddings*."

"What?" Marcie shook her head as if snapping herself out of a memory. "He was, but we knew each other from before. Marcus and I had actually gone to college together. I didn't advertise the fact because I thought it might look like nepotism, but he was in a tough spot after being fired by your friend."

I didn't point out that Marcus had been fired for sending proposals to clients on Richard's behalf laden with profanity. I also didn't point out he'd been lucky firing was the only thing Richard had done to him.

"So you gave him a job as your assistant," Kate said, prodding the woman to keep talking.

"It seemed like the perfect solution." Marcie didn't look at us as the words seemed to spill out of her. "He needed a job. I needed an assistant. We knew everything about each other, so I wouldn't have to worry about training someone. It was ideal."

"Until yesterday," Kate said.

"I'll never forgive myself." Marcie put her hands to her cheeks. "If Marcus hadn't been working for me, he never would have eaten the poisoned chocolate. It's my fault he's dead."

Kate put an arm around her shoulders. "It was just bad luck he ate the cherry one. If Marcus hadn't eaten it, another of your colleagues would be dead now."

Cassandra glanced around the cubbies, and I wondered if she was making a mental guess at who might have been dead if not for Marcus. Her eyes widened as she looked over my shoulder.

Kate's mouth dropped open as she must have noticed the same thing. "This isn't good."

I turned and came face to chest with my boyfriend. I took a step back as I noticed him glowering down at me.

"What are you doing here?" I asked.

Two uniformed officers flanked him, but I didn't recognize either.

"You took the words right out of my mouth," he said. "Do I even *want* to know what you and Tonto are doing here?"

I saw Kate open her mouth to say something about the Tonto comment, and I shot her a look. She pressed her lips together but didn't look happy about it. Kate did not appreciate sidekick cracks.

"We were just checking up on our friend Marcie," I said, trying to summon my most righteous tone of voice and putting special emphasis on the word 'friend.' "What are you and your buddies doing here?"

"Police business," he said. "We're giving your 'friend' police protection since we think she was the intended victim."

Marcie looked at the pair of officers. "Is this necessary?"

"We think so," Reese said. "The killer's attempt failed, so I wouldn't be surprised if they tried again. And the next time they might not be so subtle, and you might not be so lucky."

"No one in this office is ever eating chocolate again," Cassandra said, her eyes still wide.

"I doubt the killer will use poison again since it didn't work," Reese said, "but I could be wrong about that, so it goes without saying you should all be on alert."

Marcie cast her eyes back at her office. "I'm going to throw out every Valentine's Day gift I received."

"You got more food gifts?" Reese asked.

"Some heart-shaped cookies from another caterer, a box of artisanal honeys from a photographer, a mini cake from a baker," she said. "They arrived yesterday and this morning. I haven't touched any of them."

"She's on a diet," Kate said.

Reese nodded to one of the officers next to him. "We'll take all of that with us and test it. Please let me know if you receive anything else."

"I will, Detective." Marcie resumed chewing what was left of her thumbnail.

Reese gave a curt nod. "I'm going to leave Officer Carr with you." He turned to me. "And I'm going to walk with you out of the building."

I didn't argue. I figured we'd do enough of that once we got home.

❧ 12 ❧

Reese opened the door to our apartment and held it so I could walk inside. The drive home had been quiet, but not a lovely companionable silence. I could tell from the way he'd faced forward without looking over at me once that he was steamed. I suppose I didn't blame him for assuming I'd gone behind his back and started investigating the murder on my own. Mostly because it was true, although I had excellent reasons.

"It's not what you think," I began, then stopped myself. That wasn't entirely true. It probably *was* what he thought because by this point, Reese knew about my compulsion to solve things. "Okay, it's a little bit what you think but not why you think."

Reese rubbed a hand over his face, then sat down in the over-stuffed chair across from the couch and let out a long breath. "Enlighten me, babe."

I took a seat on the couch and tried not to get distracted by the flutter I felt every time he called me babe. "I didn't have any plans to question Marcie when the day started. Then Richard called and said he was being questioned again because the chocolatier heard him say he'd rather give Marcie hemlock. Since he'd been talking to me on the phone when he said that, I felt responsible." I took a quick breath. "Actually this whole thing is my fault since Richard didn't have any plan to give a box of chocolates to Marcie until I suggested it."

"Bringing in Richard wasn't my idea," Reese said. "You know I wouldn't knowingly do anything to make him more hysterical than he is on a regular basis."

"Richard told me it was mostly Hobbes, but he was still upset. We were just talking about who might want to kill Marcie since we know it wasn't Richard. Fern suggested if we wanted to find out the real dirt on her and any enemies she might have, we should talk to her hairdresser."

Reese leaned forward and rested his elbows on his knees. "Is this the part where Fern gave you an impromptu haircut?"

I touched a hand to my hair. I'd almost forgotten I'd had it done. "Kind of. He dragged me back to his salon, and that's when he tracked down Marcie's stylist and discovered she'd been acting jumpy lately, as if she was afraid of something."

Reese nodded. "So you thought you should question Marcie yourselves?"

"I did leave you a message," I said. "But Kate thought it would be a shame to go home without anyone seeing my new haircut."

"I know you don't think I'm going to believe you did all this to show off your hair. I'd buy it if we were talking about Kate or even Richard."

I flopped back on the couch. "Fine. I did it to help clear my best friend. And I didn't think it would hurt to make as many inroads with the city's top wedding magazine as possible."

"Both altruistic and mercenary." Reese got up and joined me on the couch. "I'm impressed. I knew you wouldn't be able to resist helping Richard, but I didn't guess you'd make it a PR mission at the same time."

"I may have been spending too much time with Richard."

He put an arm around my shoulders. "That's a given, babe."

I leaned into him, relieved he wanted to hug me and not

strangle me. "You knew I'd meddle in your case even though you made me promise not to?"

"You forget I know you, Annabelle." He kissed the top of my head. "And you've been poking around in my investigations for years. At this point, I just add it into my workflow." He mimed running a finger down a list. "Question suspects. Remind Annabelle not to meddle in the case. Get ME report. Reprimand Annabelle for meddling in the case."

I elbowed him in the ribs. "Very funny. You have to admit some of the things I've discovered have been helpful. And today I discovered the reason the killer put the poison in one truffle and not the others. The cherry cordial was Marcie's favorite flavor. Anyone who knew her well would have known that. And did you know Marcie's office lock was broken the other day? Anyone could have gotten into her office and tampered with the truffles, which makes Richard an even less likely suspect."

Reese raised an eyebrow as he rubbed his side. "I would say good work, but I don't want to encourage you. Also, the witnesses at the magazine all insist the box of chocolates sat on Marcie's desk from the time it was delivered until she gave it to her assistant."

"But they weren't there 24-7. Someone could have snuck in at night."

He raised my face so I met his eyes. "I promise to follow up on this if you'll leave the questioning of witnesses to me."

My pulse quickened as he gazed at me. "I promise as long as you promise to stop whipping Richard into a neurotic frenzy."

"Deal." He brought his lips down to mine and kissed me. When he pulled away, he ran a hand through my hair. "You can tell Kate your hair definitely wasn't wasted."

"You like it?" I asked.

"Mmmm-hmmm." He kissed me again. "I love when you wear your hair down."

A sharp series of raps made us both pull away, though it took me a moment to realize the sound came from my door. More specifically, from someone on the other side of it. Someone eager to talk to one of us.

"We could pretend we're not home," he whispered to me.

"Almost everyone who could be on the other side of that door has a key. If we don't answer, they may walk right in."

Reese muttered to himself about a locksmith and deadbolts while I stood to answer the door. Before the door was fully open, Leatrice bounded in with her arms waving.

"I can't believe what I just heard." She planted her hands on her hips and swiveled her head between Reese and me. "All this time and neither of you told me? I had to read about it in the paper. Of course, I should have heard it on my police scanner. I'm going to have to cut my shower time down even further."

Leatrice wore a head to toe red sweater jumpsuit I assumed was one of her vintage outfits, although I'd never seen it before. I reminded myself that since she was so short, she could have purchased it in the children's department. It would explain the pink heart patch pockets. She held what looked like a box of doughnuts in one hand.

"What did you read in the paper?" I asked, closing the door since it was clear her visit wasn't going to be a brief one.

"About the murder, of course." She wagged a finger at us and thrust the box at me. "Another Valentine's delivery for you."

I looked down at the box of six doughnuts from District Doughnuts and their pink and red toppings to fit the holiday. We'd used the local doughnut shop for favors for a few weddings, and I knew their creations were delicious. I also knew the last thing I needed this week was more sugar. I passed them to my boyfriend. "Don't cops love doughnuts?"

He started to give me a dirty look, then glanced at the doughnut box's clear lid. "Why yes we do." He lifted a pink glazed out of the box and returned his attention to Leatrice. "You know I'm not at liberty to discuss police matters."

Leatrice beamed at Reese. "I'm not upset at you, dear." She slid her eyes to me. "But Annabelle has always let me in on her little investigations. Once I took charge of an entire stakeout. Don't you remember?"

I felt my face flush. I'd rather Reese not remember the time I staked out a suspect and then roped my octogenarian neighbor into the scheme. "It's been crazy around here what with the upcoming wedding and all. The murder just slipped my mind."

"I can't see how, but I suppose you have been busy." She gave Reese a knowing look. "And Valentine's Day is coming up too. I'm sure you've both been busy making plans."

My cheeks got even warmer, and I avoided looking at Reese. "With my client's Valentine's Day themed wedding, I think I'm going to be over the holiday before it even arrives."

"Really?" Reese asked through a mouthful of doughnut.

I looked over at him, hoping my cheeks weren't as pink as they felt. "I was joking about that, but we don't have to . . . I mean . . ."

"I told Annabelle you two kids are welcome to join us for Valentine's Day. Sidney Allen is so romantic, you know."

Now it was Reese's turn to stammer something unintelligible, and this time it wasn't because of the doughnut.

"I already said we'd never dream of imposing on their plans," I said, catching Reese's eye until he nodded along.

"You know what they say," Reese said as he wiped a bit of pink icing from the corner of his mouth. "Four's a crowd."

"Sounds like something Kate would say," I muttered.

"Since I know about the murder, why don't you tell me about our suspects?" Leatrice perched on the arm of the couch.

I let out a nervous laugh and glanced at Reese. "I promised I wouldn't get involved in the investigation this time."

Leatrice stared at me for a moment. "And you meant it?"

Reese stifled a laugh behind his hand and stood up. "Why don't I go get changed while you two ladies discuss the case? What I can't hear won't upset me."

Leatrice craned her neck to watch him walk down the hallway to our bedroom. "I have to say, Annabelle. He really is a keeper. So considerate. You don't find that with most young men these days."

When the bedroom door closed, she produced a small notebook and golf pencil from one of her patch pockets. "So, who are our suspects?"

"To be honest," I said, "we haven't gotten very far. The person who died wasn't the intended victim, and we don't know a ton about the woman for whom the poisoned chocolate was meant."

"Did she work at the same place the victim did? *Capital Weddings* magazine?"

"She did, so our first thought was a disgruntled wedding vendor who was removed from the magazine's "Best Of" list or someone who never got on."

Leatrice gave a low whistle. "You think someone committed murder over a magazine list?"

When she put it like that, it did seem a bit ridiculous. "It's a pretty important list if you work in weddings in DC. It can make or break your career."

"The same list Richard was so upset about being left off of over the holidays?" Leatrice asked.

"Yes, but he was hardly the only person who was upset. Someone sent the editor a bunch of dead roses."

Leatrice scribbled something on her pad. "I thought weddings were supposed to be about love and happiness."

"Then it's been a long time since you've planned one," I said. "Weddings are a billion dollar business and society weddings are even more cutthroat. I wouldn't put much past some of my colleagues."

"Including murder?" Leatrice looked up from writing.

I thought about some of my fellow wedding planners. "There are some planners who'd poison their own grandmothers to get on the list."

"Maybe we should start with those then?" Leatrice licked the tip of her pencil. "Which of your colleagues are the most homicidal?"

I ran through a mental Rolodex as I thought of the people I worked with. Most were creative and cool and easygoing, but the industry certainly had its share of prima donnas and troublemakers. Some people were both.

"Why didn't I think about it earlier?" I sank back onto the couch cushion. "Richard even said he saw her when he was at the *Capital Weddings* office delivering the chocolates."

Leatrice leaned forward and almost slipped off the arm of the couch. "Who?"

"Brianna. She was desperate to get on the list and didn't. Plus, she hates Richard and would love nothing more than to cause him, and Wedding Belles, trouble. She was involved with the crazy planner who tried to ruin us a few months ago, and I was convinced she gave the woman more than a gentle nudge."

"You think she set Richard up to take the fall?"

"It would be her style," I said. "And if she was there when he dropped off the chocolates, she had opportunity."

"Did you say her name was Brianna?" Leatrice asked. "I think she was one of the people quoted in the article."

"What article?"

Leatrice waved her pencil at me. "The one I saw before I came up here. The one that goes into detail about Richard as the prime suspect in the murder. I'm pretty sure they quoted a woman named Brianna talking about him having a history of clients being poisoned."

Oh boy.

"**D**o you think Richard has seen the article?" Kate asked the next morning after I explained Leatrice's visit to her.

We were driving out to Ah-mazing Ah-melia's house in one of the nearby upscale suburbs of DC. To be fair, it was her parents' home, but she'd moved back in with them for the duration of the wedding planning. Luckily, traffic wasn't too heavy heading out of the city, because we'd purposely scheduled our visit to miss the crush of rush hour.

I stopped at a red light and held my fingers to the car's heating vents. "Have you ever known Richard to miss something like being implicated for murder in the newspaper?"

"Good point. And you said he hasn't returned your calls?"

"Nope. I left him a message last night and two this morning. I didn't mention the article but asked him to call me." I wiggled my now-warm fingers and replaced them on the steering wheel. "I'm a little worried. You know he doesn't handle stress well."

"What's the worst that could happen?" Kate asked as she checked her makeup in the passenger seat visor mirror. "He goes into hiding at your apartment again?"

"I don't think so." I let my foot off the brake as the light turned green. "Not with Reese there. That's why I'm worried. So much has changed recently--my boyfriend moved in, Richard Gerard Catering didn't make the list, his business is down, Buster and Mack pseudo adopted a baby--I'm afraid it's all too much for him."

Kate waved a hand and snapped the visor back in place. "Richard's like a cat with nine lives. He'll always land on the street."

"Don't you mean his feet?"

Kate gave a half shrug. "That too. My point is Richard has been in business for a long time. He works with brides for a living. He's used to crazy. He may be a bit freaked out right now, but he can handle this."

"I'm more afraid for Brianna," I said as the distance between housing developments lengthened, and the houses within the enclaves became larger. "Who knows what he might try to do to her?"

"What I can't figure out is why a reporter interviewed her in the first place. It's not like she has a connection to the case or to Richard. Anything she knows about him, or thinks she knows, is all secondhand information. I'm pretty sure those two have never had a conversation in their lives."

"You know Brianna," I said. "She manages to worm her way into everything. I think it's that Southern accent. People think if you have a drawl, you must be sweet."

Kate tapped a pink fingernail on the armrest. "Maybe I should start using a Southern accent. I already do an excellent Russian and British."

"Your Russian accent sounds straight out of *Rocky and Bullwinkle*," I told her.

"You wound me, sugar," Kate said in a syrupy sweet Southern drawl before dropping the accent. "I, for one, couldn't care less what happens to that awful Brianna. She's the one Richard should have given the poisoned chocolate to."

"Richard didn't give anyone poisoned chocolates, remember?"

"Well, he should have given them to her, dah-ling," she said in her Russian accent.

I shook my head as I veered right and glanced at the enormous houses set back from the road down curved driveways or perched up on sloping hills. Some looked like Tuscan villas, some looked like Georgian mansions, and others looked like a few building styles had been mashed together into sprawling yet schizophrenic estates.

"The person we should worry about is the bride," Kate said. "I'm afraid bubbly is going to morph into manic if we're not careful. Did you notice how high her voice was at the walk-through? It was like being in a meeting with Minnie Mouse on speed."

I slowed the car as I approached the Abraham's home. It was impossible to miss the massive white house with the circular drive and double stone staircases leading up to the columns framing the front door. Aside from the impressive entry, the house spread out in both directions with both an east wing and a west wing, each with a circular turret anchoring it. It was Greek revival meets English castle meets Barbie Dreamhouse.

Kate slipped her oversized sunglasses on to block the glare from the white stone. "I still say we should have had Marigold & Grey make the welcome bags for this wedding. It's not like the client couldn't afford it."

We farmed our more elaborate welcome bags out to a company specializing in custom gifts for wedding guests. The biggest upside, aside from the gifts being beautiful, was that they delivered them to the hotels. Delivering welcome bags was one of our least favorite things to do.

"You know I tried to convince them," I said, killing the engine and grabbing my purse and the broom handle from the back seat. "Amelia insisted it would be fun to make them with her bridesmaids."

"Another reason I refuse to be a bridesmaid," Kate said as she stepped out of the car and adjusted her pants so the waistband didn't fall below her hips. "The only job worse than bridesmaid is maid of honor."

We both wore black pants since I'd told Kate we'd be hauling gift bags, and even she didn't want to do manual labor in a miniskirt, although her pants were snug enough and low enough to make some of her skirts look modest. I felt grateful to have my legs covered since the weather had turned so cold, and I didn't know how Kate could stand pants that dipped so low they revealed flashes of thong. Come to think of it, I didn't know how she could stand to wear thongs.

As we started up the steps, the front door flew open and Amelia bounded out of the house, her blond hair bouncing around her shoulders. "I'm so happy you're here. I've been up since five putting the finishing touches on the bags."

"That's not good," Kate said under her breath as the petite bride jumped up and down clapping her hands.

"We can't wait to see them," I said, trying to match Amelia's energy but falling short. We followed her inside and immediately came to a halt.

The two-story foyer was filled with red gift bags, and each bag had a cluster of pink helium balloons coming out of the top.

Kate reached for my hand and dropped her voice to a whisper. "How are we going to drive with these in the back of your car?"

I did a quick mental calculation. The bags would fill my trunk as well as every inch of the back seat and possibly Kate's lap.

"Don't you love the balloons?" Amelia asked, her voice sounding like she'd been dipping into the helium herself. She hurried over and pointed to one. "I had them printed with our names and the wedding date inside a pair of hearts."

"Wow," Kate said. "I'll bet everything inside the bags is covered with hearts too."

Amelia swatted at her and giggled. "Of course." She bent over one of the bags and began producing items. "I had custom labels made for the water bottles. The mint tins are heart shaped; I picked the heart chocolates for the mini Godiva boxes; the travel candle is pink; the French macarons are red and pink; and the welcome letter is on pink heart-shaped paper."

"That's . . ." I didn't know how to finish the sentence.

"Ah-mazing," Kate said, beaming at the bride.

"Right?" Amelia gave a high-pitched trill of a laugh, and I was certain dogs all over the neighborhood were howling in pain.

"We'd better get these loaded into my car," I said, holding out the broom handle I'd brought for that very reason.

Kate took the other end and began sliding the handles of the bags over the wooden pole until we had about a dozen hanging from it.

"Isn't that clever?" Amelia's mother said as she came down one side of the sweeping staircase. "I was going to have our gardener help you, but you girls seem to have it well in hand."

"Thanks," I said to the stately blonde who was even more petite than her daughter, if that was possible. "We came up with this system a while ago."

"Did Amelia tell you we put name tags on each bag?" Mrs. Abraham asked. "We thought that would make it easier for the hotels to distribute."

I tried not to let my smile falter as I shifted the wooden pole to my other hand. Name tags would make giving out the bags twice as complicated, but I wasn't about to mention that now. It also meant we had to check each name off the hotel's rooming list when we delivered them, guaranteeing the task would take at least an extra hour.

"The tags are heart shaped." Amelia held up one pink tag with a guest's name written in red calligraphy. "Of course."

"Of course," Kate and I said in unison.

We walked back down to my car, taking small steps and keeping the pole even so the bags wouldn't slip to one side or the other. When we reached my gray CRV, I popped the trunk and we slid the bags off and into the back end.

Kate rubbed her palms, which were already turning pink from the weight of the pole. "I really hate delivering welcome bags."

"We should be able to get them all in two more trips," I said. "That's better than having to walk back and forth a dozen times, plus we don't want these balloons to deflate in the cold."

"If you say so," Kate grumbled.

My phone trilled in my purse and I pulled it out, looking down at the screen and feeling a rush of relief. "It's Richard. He's finally returning my call."

"See?" Kate said. "I told you he'd be fine. Richard is a lot tougher than he looks."

"Well, that wouldn't be hard." I answered the call and put the phone to my ear. "You finally returned my call."

"I didn't want to leave without telling you," Richard said, his voice muffled.

"Leave? What are you talking about? Where are you going?"

An impatient sigh. "I know you saw the article. If I wasn't ruined before, I am now. There's nothing left for me here, and the net is closing in."

"What net?" I asked, giving him a sigh of my own. "I told you. The police are not after you. That article was all about Brianna getting back at us."

"Even if the police don't get me, the court of public opinion is cruel." Richard's voice cracked. "I need to lay low for a while. Get out of town until things cool off."

"Have you been watching gangster movies again?"

A small yip told me Hermes was with him. "I'll be in touch once the heat is off. Don't tell anyone where I've gone."

"I don't know where you're going," I said. "Where *are* you going?"

The phone disconnected, and I looked at Kate. "We have to go find Richard before he becomes the world's most fashionable fugitive."

❄ 14 ❄

"I can't see a thing," I said, looking in the rearview mirror and seeing a sea of pink balloons behind me. We'd had to lower the back seats to get all the welcome bags in my SUV, and Kate had two at her feet.

"You're clear on this side," she yelled, her head hanging out of the rolled-down passenger side window.

I craned my own head out the window as I slowly made a left turn. "We're going to get killed before we make it downtown."

"So what's the plan?" Kate pulled her head back in and pushed aside one of the balloons in her lap. "If we hit The Wharf hotel first, we'll get rid of the most bags."

"We have to make a pit stop before the hotels." I rolled up both windows and cranked up the heat, breathing easier once we were on the Beltway. As long as I didn't have to change lanes, I could be relatively safe. I just hoped I didn't pass a cop. Driving with a car filled with balloons couldn't be legal.

"Don't tell me we're actually going to track down Richard?" Kate smoothed her hair back into place. "From what it sounds like, he could be anywhere by now."

"You know Richard," I said. "When has he ever packed in

under two hours? It takes him a day to plan what to take for a weekend away, and he spent a full week putting together outfits for our trip to Bali. No way will he be out the door so fast."

"If he's actually going anywhere." Kate adjusted her air vents so they didn't blow the balloons into her face. "It could be a bluff."

"Maybe," I said. No one could deny Richard was prone to dramatics, but he'd sounded determined on the phone. I held up my phone, which was open to the Find My Friends app. "This says he's at his offices. At least his phone is. I just want to make sure he isn't making Richard Gerard Catering HQ a pit stop as he heads out of town."

"Doesn't he know it would look bad for him if he disappeared in the middle of the murder investigation? If the press found out, they'd eat that up."

"That's why we're going to stop him before he makes a big mistake," I said. "He's not thinking straight at this point. Can you see any cars coming up in the left lane?"

Kate rolled down her window again and poked her head out. "After this blue car passes, you can go."

I watched the blue car zip by before merging into the next lane. "I think you may be right about the welcome bags. Picking them up and delivering them for clients is not the best idea."

"Not unless we get a Wedding Belles delivery van," Kate said. "Can you imagine us driving around in a white paneled van with our logo on the side?"

I shivered from the cold air and was glad when Kate raised her window. "Yep, and I can imagine Fern refusing to be seen with us."

Kate nodded. "I may be with him on that. Riding around in a delivery van would definitely hurt my street cred." She pointed at the waterfront area as we crossed one of the bridges leading into the city. "You sure you don't want to swing by the hotel first?"

"Let's just pass by the Richard Gerard offices. They're close to The Wharf area and if he isn't there, we'll do the rest of the deliveries and worry about Richard later."

I took the Twelfth Street exit ramp and turned onto Independence Avenue. Richard's company was located in Capitol Hill, an area that had gone from dodgy to trendy over the past decade. Pulling up to his town house headquarters, I glanced around and felt my heart sink. No sign of his convertible.

"He may have parked around back," Kate said, as if she could read my mind. "You know he hates to search for parking."

"You're right," I said. "Let's run inside and see if he made a stop here or if he told his office staff how to reach him."

We jaywalked across the street and hurried up the steps to the glass paned wooden front door. I didn't bother knocking, pushing my way inside and peering at the pristine living room where he met with clients and the attached tasting room where he let clients sample his food.

"Richard?" I called out. "It's Annabelle and Kate."

I started up the stairs when I heard a bark from the back of the building.

Kate grabbed my arm. "He's escaping out the back through the kitchen."

I followed her, our heels tapping on the hardwood floors as we ran, and she threw open the swinging kitchen door. Richard was halfway out the back door when he spotted us and froze, the look on his face as if we'd caught him in the commission of a crime. He wore Hermes in the black man bag slung across his chest, and the little Yorkie barked happily when he saw us.

"How did you find me?" He nearly dropped the file box in his arms.

"This is your office," Kate said. "It wasn't hard. Plus, Annabelle tracked you with her phone."

His shoulders slumped, and I noticed his black button-down was wrinkled. "Are you wearing jeans?"

Richard dropped the box to the floor. "I hoped you wouldn't have to see me like this."

"I didn't know he owned jeans," Kate whispered to me. "You're right, Annabelle. This is serious. I don't think he even has product in his hair."

I took Richard by the arm and led him to one of the stools lined up down the kitchen's granite countertops. I lifted Hermes from the man bag and handed the little dog to Kate. "Why don't you sit down and we'll talk about it?"

"What's there to talk about?" He dragged a hand through his unusually bouncy dark hair. "First I'm kicked off the list, and my business slows down. Then my attempt to fix the problem back-fires, and someone actually dies. And finally, my name is splashed all over the media as the caterer whose clients get poisoned."

Kate sat down next to him, Hermes tucked under her arm. "When you put it like that, it doesn't sound so great."

I shot her a look, then took Richard by the shoulders. "This is all temporary. What have you always told me?"

He studied me for a moment. "I tell you a lot of things. You need to accessorize more; you should start moisturizing at night; you need to stop wearing ponytails. Would you like me to continue?"

"Not those things," I said. "You've always told me that in events we're only as good as our last party. You may have had a bad run of it lately, but if anyone can turn it around, it's Richard Gerard. You cater a few fabulous parties, and no one will care about the list or the drivel Brianna told the paper."

"Who will hire me now?"

"Kate and I will for one," I said. "And you know Fern and Buster and Mack will recommend you to all of their clients."

Kate put a hand on his back. "You can probably count on Fern for some pushback against Brianna, too."

I liked imagining what salacious gossip Fern would cook up about our nemesis. Knowing Fern, it would be both creative and disturbing.

Richard squared his shoulders. "You're right, of course. I survived the Adkins diet debacle of the late nineties, not to mention the fashion of the early nineties. I can't let this take me down."

Kate's phone trilled in her pocket, and she walked a few steps away to answer it, shifting Hermes to her other hip.

"I promise the police are not focusing on you. I told Reese that Marcie's favorite type of truffle was the only one that was poisoned. And Leatrice helped me realize Brianna had opportunity and motive since she was at the *Capital Weddings* offices when you dropped off the truffles, and she hadn't made it onto the list yet."

Richard nodded. "That's right. She was steamed about it at the holiday party at the Cathedral. Do you think that's why she leaked the information to the paper?"

"I wouldn't put it past her," I said. "She may sound sweet, but she's devious."

"Are we talking about Brianna?" Kate asked as she rejoined us and slid her phone into the pocket of her snug black pants.

"You know it," I said.

"Well, I just got off the phone with one of her interns." Kate set Hermes down on the floor, and he began scurrying around sniffing at the tile. "She came to the last assistant crew happy hour, and we ended up hitting it off. She's actually too cool to be working for Brianna."

Richard shook his head. "How does that girl have interns when she barely has business?"

"Free labor," Kate said. "She has them styling Instagram photos all day. Anyway, her intern wanted to warn me."

"Warn you?" I said. "About what?"

Kate grinned. "Reese just left their offices after questioning her for over an hour."

"You know I've always liked that detective," Richard said. "I'm glad you finally decided to move things forward with him, darling."

It took all my effort not to gape at him. "I take it she thinks I have something to do with it since he's my boyfriend?"

"I don't think she singled you out," Kate said. "From what I could gather, she's vowed to ruin us all."

Richard rolled his eyes. "Then she needs to get in the back of the line."

❧ 15 ❧

"Well, that was a day," Kate said as she staggered into my apartment and flung herself onto the couch.

I was glad, for once, she wore pants since she hooked one leg over the arm of the sofa while she lay sprawled across the yellow twill cushions. True, the black pants were so tight they could have been leggings, but I'd take it.

I dropped my purse to the floor and slipped off my ballet flats, balling my toes on the rug once they were finally free from the shoes. "Tell me about it. First we convince Richard not to run off, and then we manage to get all those gift bags delivered without getting into an accident."

Kate raised her head. "There's a good chance we even got all the names matched up to the right hotel."

"You checked them off the rooming lists, right?" I'd let Kate go over the lists with the various hotel bellmen while I'd waited in front with my car. At most of the downtown hotels I'd had to double-park, and the valets had not been wild about me leaving the SUV idling under their marquees.

Kate fluttered a hand in my general direction as she reclined her head. "Sure I did, but you know how it is with weddings. Lots of guests have the same last name, and some even have the same first and last. There were three Stephen Abrahams."

"At least the bags are at all the hotels, and we can check that off our list. I think I'm going to add a clause in our contract limiting the number of hotels we'll deliver bags to. No one should have guests scattered at six different hotels."

"How many new clauses does our contract have now?" Kate asked.

"A few." I had a habit of adding a new section to our wedding planning contract every time a client did something egregious. In the last six months, I'd added clauses preventing clients from cursing at us, making us run personal errands for them, or blaming us if their guests walked off with the silverware. I imagined the Wedding Belles contract would be quite sizable within a couple more years.

I headed for the kitchen, opening the refrigerator and scanning the contents for anything quick to eat. Nothing but beverages, condiments that looked a bit worse for wear, and leftover takeout. Drat. No leftovers from Richard's dinner. I pulled out an opened bottle of white wine and reminded myself I needed to go shopping. That or find where Richard stashed the good food. I drained the last few drops of wine into two glasses, dropped the empty bottle into our blue recycling bin under the sink, and headed back out to the living room.

I handed Kate her glass. "You earned this."

"I'm assuming this comes with a fat raise." Kate took the wine and winked at me. "I'm pretty sure today should qualify me for hazard pay."

I took the chair across from her and tucked my bare feet up under me. "Every day as a wedding planner should count toward hazard pay."

Kate lifted her glass. "I'll drink to that."

I hoisted my glass before taking a sip of the cold, crisp wine. I slid back in the upholstered chair and closed my eyes. "Do you think we'll ever have a wedding that doesn't make us crazy?"

The sound of keys rattling in the lock made me open my eyes and sit up.

Reese pushed open the door and paused to take us in before stepping inside. "I take it your day was as fun as mine, ladies?"

Kate only opened one eye to look at Reese. "Did you stop someone from becoming a fugitive from justice, break about a hundred traffic laws, and get threatened by a potentially homicidal Southern belle?"

Reese raised an eyebrow. "So it was worse?"

I nodded. "Probably best not to ask."

"Agreed. I'd hate to have to arrest you both." He dropped his weathered leather bag on the floor next to my purse and came over to me, leaning down and giving me a kiss. "Although I might not mind subduing you."

I glanced over at Kate, who was smirking with her eyes closed. I was sure to hear about this later.

"My day was no picnic either," he said, walking to the kitchen. "Your friend Brianna is a piece of work."

Kate held a finger high in the air. "Not our friend. At best our frenemy. More like our nemesis."

I heard the refrigerator door open and close and the soft hiss of a bottle being opened.

Reese's head appeared above the opening between the two rooms. "You have a nemesis? I thought only supervillians and Richard had those."

I took a swallow of wine. "Let's just say there's a lot of bad blood between us and Brianna."

"And Richard and Brianna, and Fern and Brianna, and Buster and Mack and Brianna," Kate said. "You get the picture."

Reese joined us and squeezed in next to me on the chair, moving me so I was half on his lap. "I'm starting to."

"So what did she say when you asked her why she was at the *Capital Weddings* offices?" I asked, leaning against the hard muscles of his chest and trying to focus on anything but how nice they felt.

He took a swig from his bottle of microbrew beer. "How did you know I asked her about that?"

Kate waved her hands at me from the couch like you'd wave off a landing plane. She stopped as soon as Reese cut his eyes to her.

"I'm just guessing that's what you asked her," I said, feeling a little bad lying to my boyfriend.

Reese looked from me to Kate, who now wore a look of doe-eyed innocence—quite a feat for her. "The wedding industry grapevine is impressive, I'll give you that. Whoever told you what I asked Brianna must have also told you she wasn't very helpful. I can't tell you what she said, but I can tell you I doubt she had anything to do with the murder."

I let out a breath. "How can you be sure? Might I remind you this is the same woman who flirted shamelessly with you the first time you met her?"

Reese cocked his head at me. "I don't remember that."

I pushed myself up so I wasn't lying against him. "The bridal show? She batted her eyes at you so hard she nearly lost a set of lashes?"

He shook his head. "I remember you, and I remember the bartenders you had at the Wedding Belles booth wearing hot pants."

Kate perked up. "Those were my idea, you know."

"I figured," Reese said, pulling me back down to him by the belt loop of my pants.

"I can't believe you don't remember Brianna throwing herself at you. How do I know she didn't do the same today and that's why you think she's innocent?" I said. "I hope you didn't let her Southern accent fool you into thinking she's a sweet person."

"She's a pit bull in pearls," Kate said, downing the last of her wine. "And not in a good way."

"There's a good way?" Reese muttered to me.

I sat my wine glass down on the coffee table. "How can you clear her when she had motive and opportunity?"

"I haven't cleared her." Reese tucked a strand of my hair behind my ear. "I'm just telling you what my gut instinct tells me."

"I'll bet she denied sending the dead roses too," Kate said, swinging her leg down from the arm of the couch. "Although I honestly don't know if that's her style."

"What dead roses?" Reese asked.

"Didn't Marcie tell you when you questioned her?" I said. "Someone sent her a bouquet of dead roses after the 'Best Of' list came out at the end of December."

"The wedding industry version of hate mail," Kate said.

Reese sat up and nearly pitched me off the chair, catching me with one arm before I tumbled onto the floor. "She didn't mention it. Maybe she didn't think it was connected to what happened to her assistant."

"It might have slipped her mind in the aftermath of Marcus being killed," Kate said, while I readjusted myself in the chair as Reese stood up and began to pace in front of the windows.

"All of those details are important," he said. "Those roses were a clear message and might have been the beginning of escalating violence."

"The redhead in the *Capital Weddings* office said Marcie assumed it was a wedding vendor disgruntled because they didn't make it on the list or one angry they'd been removed," I told Reese.

"Like Richard," Kate added.

I narrowed my eyes at her. "But not Richard."

"I remember how upset Richard was about not being on the list." Reese stopped pacing and took a drink of beer. "Are we sure we know all the people who were kicked off the list like him?"

"Didn't we determine that the other day?" I said.

"We came up with a few people," Kate said, "but if we want to be official about it, we should compare the last few years' with this year's. I'll bet there are people who were removed a couple of years ago who still want to get back on. And the longer they've been trying, the more desperate they'll be."

I jumped up. "Sometimes you're a genius, Kate."

She grinned. "Don't tell Richard. I'd hate to ruin my reputation as a dyed with wool blonde."

I patted her on the shoulder as I hurried by her toward my office down the hall. "Your secret is safe with me."

I flipped on the overhead light in the small room that held my desk, a black swivel chair, a file cabinet, and a floor-to-ceiling bookshelf filled with client binders, wedding books, and back issues of *Capital Weddings* magazine. The room smelled of sugar from the boxes of Valentine's candy stacked against one wall, and I inhaled deeply. Even without eating any, the scent gave me a mini sugar rush. I pulled the three most recent December issues off the shelf and rushed back to the living room.

I put them on the coffee table and opened them all to the list at the back. Kate and Reese stood over my shoulder as I began scanning the names.

"Ron Tinker," I said, confirming the name of the band agent who appeared on last year's list but was missing from the updated version.

"Skyfall Video." Kate pointed as I dragged my fingers down the lists. "We were right about that one too."

"I already knew those," Reese said. "Anyone else?"

I flipped the pages of the magazines and continued comparing while Reese got the notepad and pen from his bag. "There's Petals and Petunias."

"Already have them down," Reese said.

"Wait a second," Kate clutched a hand to my shoulder. "That can't be right."

"It's right. The florist is definitely on the old list but not the new one."

"Not that." She waved a finger at the pages. "Below the florist section. Look which photographer is missing from this year's list and last year's but not the year before that."

My eyes shifted back and forth between the pages until I saw it. That couldn't be right. I twisted around and stared at her. "Maxwell Gray isn't on the last two lists."

Reese looked between us. "Why does that name sound so familiar?"

"Because he's the most notorious society photographer in the city," I said. "He also was the photographer for the wedding where we first met you."

Reese's mouth fell open. "The Pierce murder?"

"And it was his party where one of the other planners was killed last year," Kate said.

I shook my head as I rechecked the list. "He's done all the old money weddings for decades. Sure, he's as infamous for trying to seduce wedding planners as he is famous for his celebrity weddings, but I never imagined he'd fall off the list."

"It happened last year and we didn't even notice." Kate sank back on the couch. "It makes sense. There aren't as many old-school planners anymore, and he doesn't appeal to any of the newer planners. Not to mention, lecherous men are way out of style."

I felt pleased a slime ball like Maxwell finally had experienced a little karma.

"Would sending dead roses be his style?" Reese asked.

Kate and I exchanged a glance.

"For sure," I said. "He considers himself a Casanova, so something dramatic would fit his MO. Especially since he's had two years to be upset about this."

Kate clutched my arm. "Annabelle, how could we forget?"

Forget what? I thought, before the realization hit me. We'd been so focused on the decor for Saturday's wedding, we'd barely paid any attention to the rest of the team. "Maxwell Gray is the photographer for Amelia's wedding."

❧ 16 ❧

"**I** can't believe we forgot about Maxwell." I rubbed my forehead as the knowledge sank in.

"I wouldn't beat yourself up about it. Photography hasn't been the emphasis of the wedding," Kate said, emerging from the kitchen with an unopened bottle of wine and a wine opener. "I don't think it's come up again since we booked it."

I didn't comment on opening a second bottle of wine. After realizing our wedding's photographer was a likely murder suspect, we needed it. "I should have remembered the mother insisted on Maxwell. They do live in Potomac after all."

Kate peeled the foil off the top of the bottle and dropped it onto the coffee table then wedged the bottle between her knees as she screwed the wine pull into the cork. "And Amelia's mother is exactly like every client of his I've ever met. Rich and Botoxed."

Reese wrote something in his notepad. "I'll need to talk to him--and the other names you mentioned."

The cork came out of the bottle with a soft pop, and Kate fell back onto the couch, the wine still between her knees. Luckily, just a few drops splashed out and only onto her black pants. Not that my couch hadn't seen worse.

"Before Saturday's wedding?" I asked. The last thing I wanted was a photographer who was irate after being questioned by the police.

He looked up and gave me a look I recognized. "I can't put the murder investigation on hold until after your wedding, babe."

"What good is it dating a cop if he can't postpose questioning a suspect or two?" Kate mumbled as she poured Pinot Noir into both of our glasses, even though they still held traces of white wine. "Voila. Instant rosé."

Reese flicked his eyes at her, but she made a point to ignore him.

I felt a flutter of panic as I faced Kate and tried to ignore the fact that my white wine was now pink. "You did email Maxwell the wedding day timeline, didn't you?"

"Of course I did." She swirled her own glass of pink wine. "This is your usual pre-wedding jitters talking. Everyone has the timeline and the load-in details. There's nothing to worry about."

"Except the possibility our photographer is a killer," I said.

"Well, sure, there's that," Kate said. "But I feel like that's every wedding lately."

Reese flipped his notepad closed and tossed it onto the coffee table. "I promise to go easy on the guy. If I remember correctly, he's not exactly young."

Kate laughed. "Don't tell him. He's still swiping right for twentysomethings."

I wrinkled my nose. The thought of the aging photographer going after women younger than Kate made me want to gag. He still favored silk shirts worn open to the navel and cologne that arrived before he did. I took a drink of my mixed wine and was surprised I liked the slightly fruity yet still crisp taste.

"Where can I find him tomorrow?" Reese asked, heading for the kitchen with his empty beer bottle.

"He has an office around Sixteenth and U." I sat down next to Kate on the couch. "I can get the address for you as long as you promise not to throw him in jail before Saturday."

Reese's head appeared in the opening between the two rooms. "What if he's guilty?"

"If you leave me without a photographer the day before the biggest wedding of the season, for the most high-strung bride of the year, there will be two murders to solve."

Kate grinned at me. "I love it when you get fierce. That's why we call you the iron fist in the velvet glove."

"Who's we?" I asked.

She took a big gulp of wine. "No one. People. Richard. Everyone."

Reese gave me a suggestive smile. "Badass Annabelle *is* a bit of a turn on."

My face felt warm as Kate's grin grew even wider, and it was my turn to hide behind my wine glass.

"Just promise me," I said to Reese.

"I promise to put him last on my list of suspects to question." He held up his hands as if surrendering. "No brass knuckles and thumbscrews."

"Where's the fun in that?" Kate said. "Who else is on your list of suspects? You already talked to Brianna."

"I guess I might as well tell you since you'll find out anyway," Reese said. "We eliminated the band guy and the florist. Neither had opportunity and both have solid alibis. The videographer has been hard to track down, but his Instagram posts show he's shooting a destination wedding, so unless he's postdating his images, I can't see him being involved."

Kate leaned back and threw one leg over the arm of the sofa again. "Look at you using social media to solve crimes. I had no idea the police department was so hip."

"So we told you what we found out from Marcie," I said, motioning to my assistant to close her legs and getting a wink in return. "Doesn't that mean you have to tell us something you've learned about the case?"

"Quid pro quo?" Reese brushed the dark curl off his forehead. "I just told you about the suspects."

"That's not fair. A bunch of people who didn't do it isn't inter-esting." I tried to make my voice sound like Kate's did when she pouted. "Isn't there anything else you can share that wouldn't affect the case?"

His face disappeared, and I could hear the sound of cabinets opening and closing followed by a deep sigh. I wasn't sure if it was a reaction to the sad state of our pantry or my request for informa-tion on the murder case. Probably a little bit of both.

Reese appeared again, holding up the latest pizza flyer we'd gotten. "Who's in the mood for pepperoni with extra cheese?"

"Yes, please," Kate said. "Annabelle and I forgot to eat lunch again."

I could hear him calling in the pizza order before he walked back out with another beer. I stared at him as he sank into the overstuffed armchair. He finally put a hand to the side of his head. "Fine. I can tell you the type of poison used as long as you promise not to breathe a word to anyone."

"Who would we tell?" I asked.

"Richard, Fern, Buster, Mack--," Reese started to list off names.

"Fine," I cut him off. "Not even them."

"Nicotine," Reese said. "The killer injected the chocolate truffle with nicotine poison."

"Nicotine?" Kate and I both asked.

He nodded. "It's pretty easy to make. You can search it up online. You basically boil down cigarettes into a concentrate strong enough to kill someone."

"Pretty low tech," I said.

Reese frowned. "Not to mention hard to trace. It's not like buying a poison. Literally anyone could do it and cover their tracks."

"Don't e-cigarettes use liquid nicotine?" Kate asked. "You could even get cherry flavor."

"I hadn't thought about that," Reese said, "but you're right. Either the liquor in the chocolate covered the flavor of the nico-tine, or the killer got liquid nicotine that was already flavored."

"Is nicotine poisoning very common?" Kate asked.

Reese took a long swig of beer. "Not really. I don't know if I've ever dealt with a case of someone using it as a murder weapon."

Kate looked at me. "Do any of our suspects smoke?"

I thought for a moment. "I don't know, but they wouldn't have to as long as they bought the cigarettes or liquid refill."

I heard footsteps echoing in the hallway and stood up. "The pizza guy is getting really fast. I'll get plates and napkins."

As I passed the door, a shrill voice from the hallway accompanied a series of loud pounding. "Open up!"

I jumped. It wasn't the pizza guy. I couldn't tell who it was since the heavy wooden door muffled the voice, but whoever was on the other side sounded like they were in a total panic. Knowing our friends, that didn't narrow the field much.

"Sidney Allen?" I said when I threw open the door and saw the diminutive man panting in front of me. I'd rarely seen the older man wearing anything other than a dark suit with the pants pulled up high around his waist. Today was no exception. "What's wrong?"

He leaned a hand against my doorframe as he sucked in breath. "It's Leatrice."

I felt a chill go through me. "What about her? Where is she?"

Kate jumped up from the couch and joined me at the door.

"Downstairs. In her apartment." His words came out in short bursts. "On the floor."

I turned to look at Reese, but he was already right behind me.

He assessed Sidney Allen and his face became grim. "What happened?"

Sidney Allen choked back a sob. "She collapsed, and I can't revive her." He put a hand over his eyes as tears began to flow down his face. "I think she's dead."

❦ 17 ❦

"**S**he's not breathing," Richard said, looking up from where he knelt over Leatrice on the floor of her living room.

As usual, the curtains were drawn so no one could peek into her first-floor apartment, and it took my eyes a moment to adjust to the lower lighting.

"Richard," I said, noticing Hermes licking Leatrice's hand as he whined softly. "What are you doing here?"

"I was headed up to your place when Sidney Allen burst out of the apartment shrieking about Leatrice being dead. I told him to get you while I called 9-1-1 and started CPR." Richard continued chest compressions as he talked. "He was too hysterical to be any real use."

I tried to reconcile the fact that Richard was the calmest person in the room. Sidney Allen had not stopped crying during our mad dash down the three flights of stairs; Kate looked like she might faint; Reese was barking our address into his phone; and I didn't know if I was just out of breath or on the verge of hyperventilating.

Leatrice lay so still on the floor it looked like she was sleeping. Even in this state, her nearly black hair retained its flipped-up ends, and streaks of peach blush lent some color to her unnaturally pale skin. As Richard pumped her chest, the three-dimensional candy hearts attached to her pink sweatshirt quivered. I wanted to look away but couldn't.

"The paramedics are two minutes out," Reese said, jamming his phone into his jeans pocket. He got on his knees beside Richard. "You want me to take over?"

Richard shook his head without taking his eyes off Leatrice. "I don't want to stop until I get a pulse."

Kate clutched my hand, but I couldn't look at her. I knew if I saw her face, I'd fall to pieces. I took a deep breath to gather myself.

"Someone needs to stand at the front door to let the paramedics in. I'll do that." I turned to the weeping man next to me. "Sidney Allen, why don't you get Leatrice's purse? They'll need her ID at the hospital to check her in. And make sure her insurance card or Medicare information is in there."

He nodded and wandered off toward Leatrice's bedroom. I staggered into the hall, grateful to be away from the reality of what was happening and glad to have a sense of purpose. Within seconds, flashing lights pulled up outside of our building, and I held the door open as a pair of paramedics rushed inside carrying bright-orange duffels. I stayed in the hall and was joined by Kate a few minutes later.

"They've got her breathing," she said, her voice wobbly. "Can you believe Richard? I didn't even know he knew CPR."

I nodded without speaking.

Reese rushed out into the hallway. "I'm going to run upstairs, get our things, and lock up so we can follow the ambulance to the hospital." He stopped to look at me and pulled me into a hug. "They think she's going to be okay. Are you going to be okay?"

I cleared my throat enough to speak. "I'm fine. It was a shock to see her lying on the floor."

"I don't think I've ever seen her so quiet," Kate said. "She's always going in a hundred different directions and talking a mile a minute."

Reese smoothed my hair away from my face and kissed my forehead. "It's easy to forget she's over eighty."

"I guess it never occurred to me there would be a time Leatrice wouldn't be here," I said, hearing the wobble in my voice. "She's got more energy than I do."

Kate patted my back. "Don't worry. When she finally does go, I have no doubt she'll come back and haunt this building."

I couldn't help laughing. "Now there's something to look forward to."

Reese gave me a final squeeze. "Let me go upstairs and lock up. Do you two need anything aside from your purses?"

We both told him no, and he ran up the stairs two at a time. I was grateful he was thinking of all the things I wasn't. I might be used to handling stress in my job, but I was never emotionally connected to any of it. It was harder to think straight while fighting the urge to burst into tears.

The team of paramedics appeared, pushing the wheeled stretcher with Leatrice strapped in. Her eyes were still closed and her skin hadn't regained much color, but the oxygen mask over her mouth and nose told me she was alive. Sidney Allen trotted behind the paramedics with Leatrice's boxy beige purse hooked over his arm.

"You're going to Georgetown University Hospital?" I asked, knowing it was the closest one to us.

Sidney Allen bobbed his head. "I'm riding with her in the ambulance. Do you want to come with me?"

I jerked a thumb toward the stairs. "Reese is getting our things. We'll be right behind you."

He patted Leatrice's purse. "I have all her information including her power of attorney. Don't be too long. She named you the person to make any decisions for her if she can't."

I felt my knees buckle, and Kate caught me by the elbow

before I went down. "What are you talking about? I never signed anything. At least I don't remember signing anything."

Sidney Allen stopped, hiked up his pants, and took my hand. "She named you as her emergency contact, her power of attorney, and the executor of her will. You know she thinks of you like a daughter, Annabelle."

I stood with my mouth gaping open as Sidney Allen disappeared out the door. They loaded Leatrice into the back of the ambulance, and it peeled away with the siren wailing and the lights flashing. I felt a single tear roll down my cheek and heard Kate sniffle next to me.

"Don't start," she told me. "If you start, then I'll start, and it'll be a mess."

I wiped my face but still felt shell-shocked when Richard came out of Leatrice's apartment holding Hermes.

"You look like you're the one who had a heart attack," he said, sizing me up. "Don't tell me I need to do CPR on you, too, darling."

I gave my head a quick shake to snap out of my daze. "I'm fine. Just a bit startled is all."

Kate put the back of her hand to her mouth and talked behind it. "Annabelle just found out she's in charge of making all the decisions if anything happens to Leatrice."

Richard raised an eyebrow and gave my arm a brusque pat. "I don't think you'll need to worry about that tonight."

"Thanks to you," I said.

A flush crawled up his neck as he cleared his throat. "One does what one can. Now, are we going to the hospital or what?"

Kate leaned close to Richard and squinted at the corner of his mouth. "Is that coral lipstick?

Richard rubbed his lips with the back of his hand, removing the last hint of coral pink. "Before you came, I gave her mouth to mouth to try to get her breathing." He held up a finger. "If I ever find out you've told Leatrice, I will deny it and hunt you both down to the ends of the earth."

"Tell her about your heart of gold?" Kate grinned at him. "Never. Your secret is safe with me."

Reese's footsteps pounding down the stairs made us all turn. He held up a set of jangling keys. "Unless anyone wants to take their own car, I'll drive."

"Be my guest," Richard said. "I got a primo parking spot in front of the building. I may never leave."

Kate rubbed her hands together "Do you have a squad car so we can use the siren to burn through lights?"

"No, but I can put the portable light on top."

"Perfect." She glanced at me. "You know, Annabelle always says we should have one of those for wedding emergencies. Any chance of getting one authorized for civilian use?"

"Not even a sliver," Reese said.

"Let's go." I was impatient to get to the hospital and check on Leatrice. Not to mention, I was eager to find out how many documents my name was on. I looked at Hermes, who'd been unusually quiet tucked under Richard's arm. "You're bringing the dog?"

Richard pulled himself up a few inches. "I'll have you know 'the dog' is very attached to Leatrice. He'd be heartbroken to be left behind."

"The last time you tried to sneak him into the hospital, it didn't go over so well," I reminded him as I pulled Leatrice's door closed and heard the lock click into place.

"Because I didn't plan ahead." He slid his cross-body man bag around to his front and popped Hermes inside. "By now he's used to stealth mode and can stay quiet while the flap's down."

"Isn't it unsanitary to have animals in a hospital?" Kate asked, walking through the front door Reese held open.

The little Yorkie poked his black-and-brown head out of the bag and yipped.

Richard looked equally affronted. "Hermes takes more baths than some humans I know. Plus, he eats all organic so he's the picture of health."

Reese slipped an arm around me as we walked down the sidewalk. I was glad for the warmth since I didn't have my coat and for the comfort since I still felt shaky.

"You could always attach a balloon to him and make him pretend to be a stuffed animal," Kate said to Richard. "We could say we bought him in the gift shop."

From Richard's sharp intake of breath, I knew he wasn't fond of this idea. Reese used his remote to open the doors when we reached the car, walking around the front to open the passenger side for me.

"This is not how I expected to spend the evening." I paused halfway inside the car.

He shrugged. "Oh, I don't know. I've had weirder nights with your friends." He leaned his head inside as Kate and Richard piled into the back. "Worse comes to worse, I could always deputize the dog."

"Deputy Hermes," Richard said from the back seat. "I do like the sound of that."

I sighed, not knowing whether to strangle my boyfriend or hug him. I felt my phone vibrate and looked down as Reese pulled away from the curb. I recognized Sidney Allen's number from the last wedding we'd had together. He must be texting me from the emergency room, I thought as I read the single word on the screen.

Hurry.

❧ 18 ❧

I scanned the waiting room as I ran into the hospital, my nose twitching from the distinct antiseptic smell that hung in the air. No Sidney Allen, although I wasn't sure this waiting room was close to the emergency room. With the beige marble columns and dark wood, it felt more like walking into a hotel. My heart hadn't slowed since I'd gotten Sidney Allen's text, and I felt a wave of nausea as the reality of the situation hit me.

I bent over, resting my hands on my knees until the sensation passed. I turned to Kate and Richard as they walked in and motioned to some armless chairs. "Why don't you wait while I see if she's been admitted yet?"

Richard eyed the upholstered chairs. "If you think I'm touching a thing in here, you're out of your mind. Hospitals are breeding grounds for illness, and I'll bet those chairs are teeming with staph infection."

Kate stopped mid walk to the chairs and her eyes grew large.

"Ignore him," I told her. "But it wouldn't hurt to use some of Richard's hand sanitizer."

He already had the clear plastic bottle out and was squeezing gel into his hands. He held the bottle over Kate's hands and then mine without asking. I rubbed the cool gel into my palms and smelled the alcohol as it evaporated on my skin.

"If you aren't going to sit down, why don't you two stand awkwardly in the middle of the room?" I said. "Reese will be in from parking the car and can join you in a second."

I rushed over to a desk where a nurse with dishwater blond hair scraped back into a severe ponytail sat behind a monitor. "Has a Leatrice Butters been admitted? She should have been brought in by ambulance a few minutes ago."

The nurse didn't look up as she typed something into her computer. "Looks like she's in triage. You won't be able to see her until she's admitted."

"Do you know how long that will take?"

The woman glanced up at me. "No idea. We aren't too busy tonight so . . ." She let her words trail off.

"Is this the closest waiting room to the emergency room?" I asked, knowing how spread out the hospital was and how many ways you could enter. "I need to locate the man who came in with my friend."

Her eyes returned to her keyboard. "Nope." She waved a finger in a vague direction. "You want to go down that hall and walk all the way down until you almost reach the chapel and then turn left."

"Thanks." I returned to Kate and Richard as Reese walked in. "We need to go down this hall to find the emergency waiting room."

Richard rearranged his man bag, and Hermes gave a tiny yip. The nurse looked up, and Kate and I began coughing to cover the sound.

"Honestly," Richard said, "you two sound like you need to be admitted. What did I tell you about germs here?"

Reese shook his head and started taking long strides down the hall. "I don't want to be anywhere near you all when security drags Richard off."

Richard ran to catch up with him, holding the bottom of his

bag to keep Hermes from jostling. "They'd never do that with a DC cop by my side. A detective no less. You're my get-out-of-jail-free card."

Reese sized up his bulging and wiggling leather bag. "Don't count on it. I'm working hard enough to keep you out of actual jail."

Richard blanched and stopped walking. I came up behind him and put an arm around his shoulders. "Reese is joking. He knows you're innocent. Not of bringing your dog into the hospital. Obviously you're guilty of that. But not the murder."

A passing orderly nearly dropped his clipboard.

"You're such a comfort, Annabelle," Richard said.

I spotted Sidney Allen standing at a reception desk as we rounded a corner. Leatrice's purse dangled from the crook of his arm, and he had one finger pressed into the earpiece of his headset.

"I thought he only wore that to weddings," Kate said from behind me.

We were used to the entertainment diva running around at events barking orders into his headset, but it seemed out of place in a hospital. I wondered who he needed to coordinate on a Friday night in the ER.

When he saw me, he smoothed a hand across his thinning hair and let out a breath. "There you are." He tapped his earpiece. "I've been calling you."

I dug in my purse for my phone. When I pulled it out, I saw I had several missed calls. "Sorry. It was set to vibrate only. How's Leatrice?"

Tear tracks marked his doughy cheeks, but they were no longer wet. "Stable. She's being admitted now so they can run some tests, but it looks like it was a heart attack."

"Does Leatrice have a history of heart problems?" Kate asked. "Does she take any medicine?"

I looked to Sidney Allen, feeling bad I didn't know the answer to those questions. For as much time as Leatrice spent in my apartment, I didn't know as many details about her life as I should have.

"She isn't on any medications," he said. "As far as I know, she's as fit as a fiddle."

"Clearly not," Richard said under his breath.

Sidney Allen's face fell. "No, I guess you're right. She only seemed fine. All this time she was on the verge of dropping dead." He began to sniffle.

"But she's fine," I insisted. "If there is an issue, it's been caught, and we can take steps to make sure it doesn't happen again."

Sidney Allen nodded, one hand pressed over his mouth as he turned back to the desk to answer a question from the admitting nurse.

"We're here! We're here!" Fern's voice carried across the waiting room as he ran through the glass doors. Behind him, walking as fast as their bulk would allow, were Buster and Mack. Prue, baby Merry's teenaged mother, brought up the rear with her ash-brown hair sticking out of the top of a pink knit hat with a hole for ponytails, and she carried a diaper bag over one shoulder. Mack held a plastic baby carrier with one hand, and both men were huffing trying to keep up with Fern.

I swiveled to face Kate. "When did you have time to tell them?"

"In the back seat on the way here. I have fast thumbs."

When he reached us, Fern leaned against Richard, gasping for breath. He had on a long white jacket worn open over black pants.

"Is that a stethoscope around your neck?" I asked.

"Kate said it was a medical emergency," he said between quick breaths. "You never know when this might come in handy."

"Is it just me, or does he look like he's wearing a white doctor's coat?" Reese whispered to me.

"If he starts diagnosing patients, I'll make him take it off," I said. I only hoped he hadn't gotten the jacket from an actual doctor. Fern was known to go to extraordinary lengths to get his outfits just right. The real giveaway he wasn't a doctor, aside from the huge topaz ring on his finger, were the rhinestones decorating the metal bits of the stethoscope. Leave it to Fern to "bling out" his medical accessories.

"How is Leatrice?" Buster asked, his deep voice echoing off the tile floors.

"Heart attack," I said. "Sidney Allen says she's stable and being admitted."

"The poor dear." Fern produced a monogrammed linen handkerchief from his pocket and dabbed at his eyes. "I can't believe it. She always seems so full of life."

"We activated our prayer chain on the way over," Mack said. "You now have all the members of the Born Again Biker Church praying hard for her recovery."

This brought on a whole new flood of tears for Sidney Allen, who had rejoined us, so Fern passed off his handkerchief and whipped out another identical one for himself.

Sidney Allen took the linen square and wiped his eyes. "She would be so touched you're here. She thinks of all of you as her family."

Mack began to sniffle, and I felt tears prick the backs of my own eyes. I wondered how many more handkerchiefs Fern had in his pockets.

"We should all be thanking Richard." Reese clapped him on the back. "If it hadn't been for his quick thinking and doing CPR, she might not have made it."

Everyone stared at Richard, and he looked at the floor. "I only did what anyone would do."

"Nonsense." Fern flung his arms around Richard, pulling him into a hug so hard Richard squeaked. "You're a hero."

Fern released him, and Richard staggered back. Hermes poked his head out of the man bag, sniffed the air, and ducked back into the bag.

Prue's mouth opened. "Was that a . . .?"

"Nope," I said. "It definitely wasn't."

Richard smoothed the front of his dove gray jacket and looked eager to change the subject. "How did you all get here anyway? I know you didn't put the baby on the back of your motorcycles."

"We were still at the studio getting ready for tomorrow, so we hopped into one of the floral vans and swung by Fern's salon on the way," Mack said.

"It was all very exciting," Fern said. "I've never jumped in the back of a white van before."

"That does sound . . . " I began.

"Creepy?" Kate muttered so only I could hear her.

Fern giggled. "They barely slowed down, and I had to run alongside the van for a few steps."

"Sometimes when we stop this particular van, it doesn't like to restart right away," Buster explained.

"Sounds like a car you'd have, Annabelle," Richard said.

I made a face at him. "Not anymore. My old car is history."

"Someone burned it to the ground," Kate said, winking at Prue. "Molotov cocktail. If I'd known that was all it took to get Annabelle to buy a new car, I would have thrown one myself."

Prue's head swung back and forth as she followed the conversation, her blue eyes unblinking, and I hoped we weren't terrifying her. Reese pulled his phone out of his jeans and looked at the screen, stepping away from our group to answer it.

"When can we see her?" Buster asked Sidney Allen.

"I don't know," he said, handing a soggy handkerchief back to Fern. "Let me check with the nurse and get her room number."

He walked over to the desk while Fern held the wet linen in front of himself with two fingers.

"I'm going to search for a vending machine. I'm starving. We never did get our pizza," Kate said as she wandered off.

I almost slapped my forehead. We'd left before the delivery guy had arrived with our pepperoni with extra cheese, and it had completely slipped my mind. I'd have to call the restaurant to apologize once I got home.

"What should I do with this?" Fern asked in a stage whisper, still holding the used handkerchief like it was nuclear waste.

Prue dug through the diaper bag on her shoulder and held out a pink plastic bag. Fern raised an eyebrow.

"A dirty diaper baggie," she said.

His eyes lit up. "Brilliant." He dropped the wet handkerchief in the bag and tied the flaps into a knot.

Reese pulled me aside. "I'm really sorry, babe, but I have to run. It's work. Can you get a ride home?"

"Of course. I'll call a Lyft or catch a ride with Buster and Mack provided the van starts again." I noticed his furrowed brow. "Is everything okay?"

He kissed me on the cheek. "It's fine. Call me if anything changes with Leatrice."

He walked down the hallway toward the far entrance as Kate returned empty handed.

"No luck?" I asked.

She frowned. "Not yet. They must be hiding the sugar so people won't binge candy bars while they wait. I guess we're Ubering home since Reese has to go talk to his captain about the coroner's report?"

"You overheard him on the phone?" I was partly annoyed and partly pleased.

"By accident," she said. "And he didn't say much. Just something about the evidence not matching up with the coroner's report on Marcus."

"That's odd."

"Your boyfriend thought it was more than odd. He said the murder couldn't have happened the way he thought it did."

❧ 19 ❧

"This doesn't feel right," Kate said as we walked down the sidewalk on U Street the next morning.

It was early enough that the trendy restaurants and clubs were still shuttered from the night before, and only a handful of coffee shops and cafes had their doors open and sandwich boards set out in front. The scent of stale beer was thankfully overpowered by the aroma of coffee, making me wish we had time to stop and grab a hot mocha.

"I know how you feel, but there's nothing we can do at the hospital right now. Visiting hours aren't until the afternoon, and Sidney Allen was hoping to bring her home today anyway." I put my arm through Kate's as we navigated the uneven pavement. "Besides, Leatrice would love nothing more than to know we were soldiering on with the investigation in her stead."

"Speaking of things that will make your boyfriend have his own heart attack, did you tell him we were making a pit stop to talk to one of the suspects?"

"The way I figure it, Reese's partner went out of town, so he might appreciate the assist. Plus, if we clear Maxwell for him, he won't have to bother questioning him later."

I'd been more than a little pleased to hear Hobbes had taken a few vacation days, even though Reese hadn't been thrilled. For him it meant more work. For me it meant a friendlier face in the police department for Richard.

Kate stopped us in front of the arched brick entryway I recognized from the last time we'd been to the photographer's studio. "I'm sure he'll appreciate that reasoning."

I ignored her sarcasm as I punched in the code to Maxwell's unit and waited to hear his voice on the speaker. Instead, the door buzzed open.

"He must be expecting someone." Kate tugged at the wooden door. "I guess ten isn't too early to meet with a photographer."

"I wish more of our clients would agree to morning appointments," I said as I ducked into the small foyer and felt an immediate blast of heat. "The after-work meetings are starting to get really old."

Kate eyeballed the stairs and slipped off her heels. "He's on the fifth floor, isn't he?"

I nodded, feeling glad I'd worn my usual flats. "He's going to be surprised when he sees us. I wonder who he's actually expecting."

We trudged up the stairs, stopping halfway to catch our breath, until we stood in front of a shiny black door with a gold name plate on the front that read "Maxwell Gray, Master Photographer" in swirling etched letters.

"We are definitely at the right place," Kate said, taking shallow breaths and leaning against me as she put her shoes back on. "Every other door in this place is plain wood."

I put a finger to my lips as I knocked. Within moments it was thrown open, leading me to believe he'd been waiting right on the other side of it. He was eager to see whoever he thought we were, and from the expression on his face as he stood holding the door, it definitely wasn't us.

Maxwell Gray looked exactly as he always had. Long flowing blond hair that looked like it had been professionally blown out, a slightly orange glow that could only result from a spray tan, and enough exposed chest to scandalize Kate. He usually wore silk shirts with wide collars, but today he had a red satin robe belted over his black pants. I knew it was only a matter of time until he morphed into Hugh Hefner.

He blinked quickly a few times. "Did we have . . ."

"An appointment?" I tried to make my laugh sound genuine as Kate and I barreled past the stunned man. "No, but we knew you wouldn't mind if we dropped by to discuss Amelia's wedding with you since it is tomorrow."

Maxwell regained his composure like a cat landing on his feet. "Not at all, ladies. Come right in." He reached in for air kisses that were more lips than air. "What can I get you to drink? Mimosas?"

"I wouldn't say no to a--" Kate started to say before I elbowed her.

"No mimosas today. We have a busy day of wedding prep ahead of us," I said more to Kate than to him. "Not to mention the wedding rehearsal and rehearsal dinner."

"Another time then." He led us further into the open space of his studio, which had high ceilings, dark hardwood floors, and soaring windows letting in the morning light.

The only other time we'd been here had been at night, so I hadn't noticed the view. Since DC wasn't a city of skyscrapers, a fifth story could look over quite a few streets, and I saw the rooftops of nearby houses as well as the stone-columned Masonic Temple building a few blocks away.

Maxwell waved us toward a grouping of chrome-and-black-leather couches around a glass coffee table that held stacks of wedding albums. "You're sure I can't get you some coffee at least?"

"That would be lovely," Kate said in a rush then lowered her voice. "You owe me since you didn't let me stop for coffee on the way."

"Fine," I whispered to her. "But if he makes them Irish, don't drink it." I raised my voice. "Two, thank you."

Maxwell headed to a wet bar setup against one wall. "I only do espresso. I hope that's okay."

"It's perfect," I said, perching on the edge of one of the boxy couches.

This minimalist studio was a far cry from his old office, which had been decorated in mid-century sultan with rich colors and lots of sumptuous fabrics. I much preferred this simple look, even though the boxy leather furniture wasn't as comfortable.

"How are you enjoying the new space?" I called over to him as he fiddled with his small chrome espresso machine.

"I love being able to live and work in the same location," he said over his shoulder. "I don't have to reign in my creativity anymore."

From the rumors I'd heard about Maxwell, he'd never reigned in much. I'd never found male cleavage enticing, especially when covered with so much coiffed chest hair, but someone must because he'd earned a reputation as a ladies man with a particular talent for seducing wedding planners. I shuddered every time I thought about it.

"So this isn't just your office?" Kate asked.

"No." He gave us what could only be called leering smiles as he approached, holding out two white espresso cups with lemon peel twists curled up in the saucers. "My bedroom is down the hall."

I took the small cup and tried to return his smile without gagging.

He took a seat on the couch across from us and stretched his arm along the back, letting his robe sag open. "What did you want to discuss about Amelia's wedding? I got the timeline from Kate earlier." He winked at her. "Thank you, my dear."

I glanced at my assistant. We hadn't discussed exactly what issue to bring up with Maxwell since there were no problems. We also hadn't planned out how to casually work Marcie into the conversation. I took a small sip of the rich espresso as I thought of what to say.

"The shot list," Kate said, crossing her legs so the high slit in her skirt showed off most of her thigh. "We know you already have one for the portraits, but we wanted to go over all the details we need to have photographed. There are lots of Valentiney elements, and the bride would like this wedding to be submitted to a magazine."

"Of course." Maxwell sat up, his eyes not leaving Kate's legs. "You know I'll do anything to help."

Most of the time Kate's low necklines and short hemlines made me crazy, but sometimes they came in handy. My own purple sheath dress wasn't much help since it reached my knees and had no thigh-high slit, not that I had any desire to flash Maxwell some leg.

I saw my opening and downed the rest of my espresso before setting the cup onto the coffee table. "We'd love your input on which magazine. You have so much experience, you must have connections with the top publications."

His sultry smile slipped for a second before he flopped back on the couch and stretched out like he was sunning himself. "I think we should go national. Why bother with local magazines when we have the world at our disposal?"

"So no *Capital Weddings?*" I asked, already feeling a jolt from the shot of super strong coffee. "I thought you used to have lots of weddings featured in there."

He jerked up. "Unfortunately, loyalties change too quickly in this town. I used to be very friendly with the magazine's editor, but she left."

I didn't want to know Maxwell's definition of friendly, but I had my suspicions.

"What about this new editor?" Kate asked, her voice betraying no hint that she knew anything about Marcie.

Maxwell ran a hand through his mane of blond hair, and I noticed a few flashes of gray in the sunlight. As my eyes drifted from his hair to the faint sunspots on his hands, I felt a moment of sympathy for the photographer. Getting old must not be easy when you'd built a business on your own sex appeal. I doubted he had many more years where he could count on seducing his way to more clients.

"A lost cause," he said. "She's only interested in the flavor of the month, and with photographers there are hundreds to choose from."

"That must be upsetting." Kate leaned forward and rested her elbows on her knees. "Especially after all the years you've put into the wedding industry."

Maxwell leaned forward as well. "Did you know she had the nerve to remove me from the list?"

Kate recoiled in mock horror. "No! You've been on the list for years."

"Decades," Maxwell corrected. "At first I was livid, but I'm not the only veteran she kicked off."

"Our friend Richard Gerard was also removed," I said. "He was pretty upset."

"It's a travesty." Maxwell twirled a finger in his fluffy chest hair while he spoke. "Some of the people on the list now barely know what they're doing. They're children."

It was true the list was skewing younger, although I couldn't complain too much since Kate and I could be considered part of that trend.

"Did you ever have the urge to get back at her for kicking you off?" I asked, lowering my voice.

Maxwell stopped twirling. "You mean revenge?" He narrowed his eyes at me before shaking his head. "Why bother? The way editors come and go over there, I just need to wait until the next one takes her place."

I'd never thought of that. He was right that *Capital Weddings* had had a lot of editorial turnover in the past few years. It was part of the reason I'd never met the last editor and only recently met Marcie. Waiting for her to be replaced wasn't the worst strategy, although who was to say he hadn't wanted to speed up the process? Wanting a new editor was a pretty good motive for wanting the current one out of the picture, although I had a hard time picturing Maxwell plotting murder. Sending dead roses to scare her wasn't off the table though.

"Do you have any reason to think the editor will be leaving soon?" I asked.

He gave a less than convincing shrug. "How would I know something like that?"

The door to his studio opened and closed, and all our eyes swiveled to the sound of heels tapping on the hardwood.

"I'm here, big boy." A woman's voice called out, echoing off all the glass and metal. "I hope you're ready for me."

When the redhead from *Capital Weddings* came into view--her face as stunned as ours no doubt were--I had a pretty good idea why Maxwell might think Marcie would be leaving the magazine.

⚜ 20 ⚜

"I didn't . . . I mean . . ." The woman's face was as red as her hair as she stood with her black trench coat partially undone.

Kate jumped up and went over to her, tugging the coat closed again so we didn't have a full view of her sheer lace lingerie underneath. "You'll thank me later."

When she sat back down, I gave Kate a questioning look.

"I've had a few trench coat meet ups go wrong," she said. "I feel her pain. At least she had on something underneath. You don't want to know about the time I was supposed to meet a guy at the National Archives. Let's just say you do not want to be walking up those steps when it's windy and the only thing under your coat is— well, you can imagine the rest."

"Unfortunately I can," I said, turning my attention back to the woman in the trench coat.

Maxwell stood and walked over to her as if there was nothing out of the ordinary. To be fair, for him there probably wasn't. "Cassandra, darling. I was expecting you earlier."

"Traffic," she managed to say with a look over his shoulder at us. "I didn't think you'd have company."

Maxwell fussed with the collar of her coat. "These ladies are the planners for my wedding this weekend. Do you know Wedding Belles?"

"We've met," I said. "At the *Capital Weddings* offices the other day. I didn't know you two knew each other."

Cassandra blushed and looked down. "Maxwell reached out to us before the holidays. Marcie wasn't available, so he ended up taking me to lunch."

It didn't take much to figure out Maxwell had set his sights on one of the other editors when he'd had no luck with Marcie. I also felt sure this visit had taken place after the list came out and he'd been excluded again.

"Something about Cassandra drew me to her." Maxwell brushed a lock of red hair off her face as he gazed down at her. "Our connection was electric."

Kate shifted next to me, and I guessed she felt like as much of a voyeur as I did. I hoped Maxwell remembered we were still in the room.

"Maxwell was telling us about his plan to wait until Marcie leaves the job," I said, taking a breath before making a stab in the dark. "I'm assuming the plan to scare her off with the dead roses was your idea, Cassandra?"

She met Maxwell's eyes and her own held a look of betrayal. "You know that was your idea. I told you she wouldn't be spooked by something so silly."

Maxwell's shoulder drooped, and he turned around to face me. "How clever of you." He stepped away from Cassandra, giving her a backward glance as he returned to the couch. "I never mentioned the roses to them."

Pink blotches appeared on her fair cheeks. "It was harmless. Maxwell thought it would give Marcie the push she needed. She shouldn't have had that job anyway."

"Why not?" Kate asked.

"I was next in line for promotion. I've been working as an associate editor for three years. I know everything about the magazine. But they brought Marcie in and she's clueless. She doesn't know anything about weddings."

Kate gave me a look. One of our constant complaints about *Capital Weddings* was the staff knew little about the actual ins and outs of wedding planning.

"So Marcie stole your job, and when Maxwell came along as eager to get rid of her as you, it was easy to go along with it, right?" I asked.

"Like I said, it was harmless. Dead roses didn't do anything but smell up the office and freak her out for a few minutes. Marcus convinced her it was nothing to worry about."

"So you had to step it up?" Kate said. "Did you and Maxwell conspire to kill Marcie together?"

Maxwell sat bolt upright. "Kill her? What are you talking about?"

Cassandra shook her head so hard I thought her hair might fly off. "We never talked about killing her. That wasn't us. Besides, I ate one of those chocolates."

"If you poisoned them, you'd know which one not to eat," I said. "Only the one Marcus ate was poisoned."

She closed her eyes briefly as if absorbing the information. "Why would I want to kill Marcus? It's not like I want to be Marcie's assistant. I'd rather slit my own wrists than do that."

It sounded like Cassandra really didn't like her boss. This painted quite a different picture than the one she'd given us of a devoted employee when we'd first met her.

"You wouldn't have known that Marcie wouldn't eat the chocolates," I said. "Killing Marcus wasn't something you meant to do."

Cassandra crossed her arms over her chest. "Of course I would have known Marcie wouldn't touch those truffles. She was on a diet."

I tried to think back to when Marcie had told us at the *Capital Weddings* office. Had Cassandra been there for that part of the conversation? "You knew about her diet?"

"It's not a huge office space," she said. "No one can keep secrets for long around that place."

That did poke a hole in my theory, along with both her and Maxwell's genuinely shocked expressions. I knew the photographer was a skilled seducer, but it was harder to fake actual shock.

"So you're telling us you two teamed up to send the dead flowers, but you had nothing to do with the fact someone tried to knock off your boss for good?" Kate asked. "That seems hard to believe."

"I swear," Cassandra made a criss cross over her chest. "I may have wanted her job, but I wouldn't have killed her to get it."

Kate stared her down. "What about Marcie's broken lock? Was that part of the plan to freak her out too?"

"No," Cassandra said. "That wasn't either of us. I don't know who did it."

Kate made a noise in the back of her throat indicating she wasn't so sure.

"And you wouldn't have killed to get back on the list?" I asked Maxwell.

"Don't be absurd." Maxwell stroked his own chest hair as he spoke. "I am a lover of women. Not a killer of them."

I kept my eyes on his, as much to avoid having to glimpse his exposed chest as to assess his honesty. I hated to admit it, but I didn't think he was lying. I also didn't think he had it in him to murder someone. Knowing Maxwell, he hadn't eliminated the chance he could get his claws into Marcie eventually.

"You aren't going to tell Marcie are you?" Cassandra asked.

"You're going to have to talk to the police," I said, not answering her original question. "Tell them everything you told us."

Cassandra nodded. "I do want to help find out who killed Marcus. Like I told you earlier, he was always nice to me. Nicer than Marcie, especially when he let juicy tidbits about her slip out."

"If you like to hear juicy gossip about bosses, you should come to the assistant happy hours," Kate said, then added quickly, "not that I ever share anything like that about my boss." She tapped a finger to her chin. "Actually, I've never had any juicy details to share until recently, but I'm hoping now that she has a hot boyfriend I'll . . ." Her words drifted off when she saw me eyeing her, and she slapped my knee. "Of course I'm kidding. My lips are sealed." She darted her eyes to Cassandra. "I'll text you the details later."

"Was there anything else, ladies?" Maxwell stood. "I'm assuming this was all a ruse to interrogate me."

I didn't attempt to convince him otherwise. He may be slimy, but he isn't stupid.

"I hope this won't affect this weekend's wedding," I said. "I was being honest when I said Amelia wants to get it featured in a magazine."

Maxwell didn't look back as he led us to the door. "I would never let anything come between me and creating beautiful images for my clients. Not even a wedding planner trying to frame me for murder."

That wasn't comforting.

"I wouldn't say we were trying to frame you for murder," Kate said. "You did a pretty neat job of incriminating yourself. You know what they say, if it walks like a schmuck . . ."

Maxwell wrenched open the door and held it open for us without speaking. I flinched as he slammed it shut behind us. Not exactly the way I'd envisioned that meeting going, although I never could have anticipated a woman walking in wearing a trench coat and little else. I only hoped he was true to his word and wouldn't make our lives miserable at the wedding, although knowing divas the way I did, I couldn't count on it.

"I think you were right," I said as we started down the stairs. "Talking to him before the wedding wasn't the greatest idea."

"Don't worry." Kate pulled off her heels at the first landing.

"He wouldn't dare tick off a Potomac mother. Chances are he's sleeping with her."

I laughed in spite of myself. "Thanks, Kate." I paused to wait for her. "FYI, it's 'walks like a duck' not 'walks like a schmuck'."

Kate gave me a wicked smile. "Oh, I know."

❧ 21 ❧

"From the cheesiest person in town to the bubbliest," Kate said as we made our way down the corridor of The Wharf Intercontinental Hotel, the plush carpet making our walk nearly stealth.

Amelia had checked in the day before the wedding so she could use the suite to get ready for her rehearsal dinner and not have to worry about unpacking on the wedding day. I'd made the mistake of telling her we'd check in on her once she was in her room, and I had gotten a text from the bride as soon as we'd driven away from Maxwell's studio.

"I still find it odd he's shooting her wedding," Kate continued. "I felt sure she'd go for one of the natural light photographers."

"You might have been right about the mother. She was adamant about hiring him."

Kate made a face. "Mrs. Abraham fits the Maxwell mold—Botoxed and bleached blond."

I put a finger to my lips as we approached the suite at the end of the hall. It wouldn't do to have our client overhear us refer to her as "Botoxed" even if her forehead hasn't moved in a decade.

I rapped my knuckles on the door and was surprised when it wasn't the bride who opened it. "Fern? What are you doing here?"

"What do you think, sweetie?" He waved us in. "Amelia decided she wanted her hair done up for the rehearsal dinner."

His dark hair was pulled up into a high man bun, and he wore tailored white pants with a matching three-button jacket over a cherry red shirt. On anyone else I would have thought a white suit was a dangerous choice--especially since he did hair--but Fern managed to stay spotless no matter how much he snipped or how much product he spritzed. He held a hairbrush in one hand and a bottle of high-end styling product in the other. He waved the brush at us. "Nice coordination, lovelies."

I glanced at Kate and noticed for the first time that her blouse was lavender, which went with my purple dress. Leave it to Fern to notice something neither of us had all morning. "You know us," I lied. "Always thinking ahead."

"Is she here?" Kate peered around the living room of the suite, her heels tapping on the pale wood floors.

Fern shook his head and his bun bobbled. "She let me in then said she had to run out and get a latte before I started on her updo."

Kate sat down onto the gray couch and leaned back against one of the cobalt-blue throw pillows. "I still think it's absurd that we're here. Why does the bride need us to watch her get ready? Won't we have enough togetherness tomorrow? We will be with her for about twelve hours."

"I agreed to calm her down during one of her manic moments," I said. "We don't have to stay the whole time. We'll just get a little face time, make sure she doesn't have any changes to the timeline, and leave for The Hay-Adams."

Fern leaned against a sleek, dark wood desk. "What's at The Hay-Adams? I thought the wedding was at a church and the reception was back here."

"The groom's parents picked the rooftop of The Hay-Adams for the rehearsal dinner," Kate told him. "Annabelle thinks they were trying to outdo the bride's parents with an even better view than the Potomac River at sunset."

"It's hard to beat the view of the White House from the Top of the Hay," I said.

"How snarky." Fern arched a brow. "I love it. Any chance of a catfight between the families tomorrow?"

"Nope," I said. "Both families have enough money to make all their aggression extremely passive."

Fern poked out his lower lip. "Too bad. I haven't had any good gossip lately. At least nothing I hadn't started myself. I need something yummy to tell Leatrice when I visit her. You know how she loves my stories."

"You're going to see her at the hospital?" I asked.

"She got sent home." Fern swiped his eyes with the back of his hand. "The dear is apparently much better and wanted to recover at home. Sidney Allen is with her."

I blinked away the tears of relief that welled up in my eyes. "That's great news."

"I almost forgot. We do have something juicy for you," Kate said. "Maxwell Gray is the one who sent the dead roses to Marcie with help from Cassandra. They wanted to scare her out of the position because Cassandra wanted her job, and Maxwell wanted to get back on the list."

"No!" Fern nearly dropped his brush then angled his head at us, tapping the bristles on his thigh. "Who's Cassandra?"

"She works at *Capital Weddings*. She'd been vying for the head editor position before Marcie came along," I said. "Redhead."

Fern's eyes narrowed. "Natural red or some burgundy crime against hair?"

"Natural," Kate told him.

Fern seemed satisfied with that answer. "I'm assuming she and Maxwell are . . .?" He wiggled his eyebrows suggestively, although when talking about Maxwell that really wasn't necessary, and I told him so.

"I don't want to be indiscreet, sweetie," he said, when we both knew indiscretion was his middle name.

"I'm pretty sure he was using her to get back in the magazine's good graces," I said. "I feel a little sorry for her."

"I feel sorry for anyone involved with Maxwell." Kate rubbed her arms and shivered. "He's so old."

"Forget old," I said. "He's so cheesy. I can't believe anyone still falls for exposed chest hair and Fabio-style feathered bangs."

"DC's a tough town for dating, Annabelle," Kate said. "Cassandra could do worse."

I didn't see how, but I let it go. When it came to dating in DC, Kate was the expert.

"So I assume Maxwell and this Cassandra woman are at the top of the suspect list now," Fern said. "Is anyone else on there with them?"

I slapped my leg. "I almost forgot. Brianna was at the *Capital Weddings* offices when Richard dropped off the chocolates, so Reese questioned her."

Fern took the spot next to Kate, his eyes wide, and dropped the brush and styling product onto the cushion beside him. "I'll bet she loved that."

"It serves her right after the quotes she gave the newspaper about Richard," I said.

Fern ping-ponged his head between us. "What quotes? What paper? Why did you not call me about all this?"

"Brianna took it upon herself to tell the media Richard has a history of clients dying from poison," I said. "You can imagine how he reacted."

Fern made tsk-ing noises in his throat. "I assume he's applying for asylum in another country by now?"

"Come to think of it, we're lucky Brianna didn't tell the paper *we* have a history of clients being poisoned," Kate said.

"Don't be so sure she didn't," I said, "but the reporter would have cut it since it isn't relevant to this murder case."

"She might not have wanted to come after you two after what

happened the last time." Fern smiled and rested both hands on top of his knee.

"I don't know if you'll be able to come up with anything as good as convincing the world she's a madam," I said.

Fern rubbed his hands together. "Challenge accepted."

"It might be time for some fresh and freaky rumors, because it seems like she's gotten over any hesitation to come after us," Kate said. "After the police questioned her, she told everyone in her office she was going to ruin all of us."

Fern pressed a hand to his heart. "Me included?"

Kate nodded. "All of us. She thinks we're all behind the tables being turned on her and her becoming a suspect in Marcus's murder."

"I wish I could take some credit for it, but this time I'm completely innocent," Fern said. "Do the police think she did it?"

I sighed. "No. Reese thinks she's innocent, but not only did Brianna have opportunity, she had motive. She'd been trying to get on the list and still didn't make it this year."

"As far as motives go, that isn't the strongest one I've heard." Fern stood and beckoned for us to follow him into the bathroom where his styling supplies were arranged on the ivory marble countertop. I stood in the doorway and admired the oval freestanding tub against the far wall and the glass shower next to it.

"Way to burst our bubble," Kate said.

"I'm just saying I know of a couple of people who have stronger motives." Fern patted the stool in front of the mirror and pointed at me. "You haven't touched your hair since I did it, have you?"

"Which people?" I asked, sitting on the stool and making a point not to answer his question about my hair. "And don't you dare say Richard."

"Really, sweetie." Fern shook his head at me as he began running his fingers through my hair. "Give me a little more credit. I meant her hairstylist and her ex-husband."

"Her hairstylist?" Kate leaned over to examine Fern's serums and sprays arranged in a neat row, picking up one and reading the label. "The one who told you she'd been acting nervous?"

Fern plucked the bottle from Kate's hand and squirted a white gel into his palm. "I dug a bit further and got the real story. Apparently Marcie had been getting free cuts for the past year with the promise she'd get her hairdresser on the 'Best Of' list."

"Let me guess," I said, "Marcie didn't come through."

Fern rubbed his palms together and started working the gel through the back of my hair from the underneath. "No list. The stylist was fuming and making lots of loud threats in the salon once the magazine hit the stands."

"Threats about killing her?" Kate asked, hopping up onto the counter to face us.

Fern twitched one shoulder. "I don't know specifics of what was said, but let's just say you can add another name to people unhappy about the list."

"And what's this about an ex-husband?" I asked as Fern fluffed my hair with both hands then fanned it out around my shoulders.

"Any ex should always be suspect number one," Kate said with a serious nod. "I can't believe we didn't know she was married."

Fern waved me up and motioned for Kate to sit on the stool. "That's why she came to DC in the first place. Following her husband's job."

Kate rolled her eyes. "Reason five hundred I'm in no rush to get married."

"How did you discover this?" I asked Fern, watching him apply a different product to his hands.

He tilted his head at me. "The stylist network knows all, Annabelle." He moved his hands together briskly before running them through Kate's hair, scrunching them as he went. "From what I heard, the divorce wasn't pretty, and she ended up getting more alimony than her ex would have liked."

"That's a pretty good motive," I said. "You don't have to pay alimony to a dead ex-wife."

"Even more incriminating?" Fern leaned down so his face was

even with Kate's as he examined her hair in the mirror. "The ex is a chef."

"You're kidding." Kate swiveled her face to look at Fern and almost bumped his nose.

"You know I never kid." Fern straightened up. "Gossip, yes. Joke about motives, no."

I pulled my phone out of my bag. "I need to tell Reese. What's the name of the ex-husband?"

Fern tapped a finger to his chin. "I think it was Symon with a 'y'."

"And where does he work?" I asked.

The door to the suite opened, and I could hear Amelia's high-pitched voice as she called out to tell Fern she was back.

"In here," Fern bellowed back then dropped his voice to a near whisper. "That's the funny thing. I was surprised Marcie came to Love Brunch knowing her ex was back in the kitchen."

I dropped the phone back into my bag and grasped his arm before he could leave the room. "Are you telling me Marcie's ex-husband is a chef at The Hay-Adams hotel?"

I looked down at Kate and noticed she looked as stunned as I felt. "Looks like our rehearsal dinner just got a lot more interesting."

Kate nibbled the edge of her lip. "Or a lot more dangerous."

❧ 2 2 ❧

"**T**his is bad," I said as I stood in the doorway to the Top of the Hay, the glass-walled ballroom on the roof of the hotel overlooking the White House. The only sound aside from the soft Muzak piped in overhead was the muffled tapping of Kate's toe on the carpet as we both inspected the room setup for Amelia's rehearsal dinner.

"I wouldn't say bad," Kate said after a brief hesitation. "It's a little simple is all."

A single rectangular table ran down the long part of the L-shaped room with a white twill cloth covering it. Instead of center-pieces, the table held a row of white pillar candles encased in straight glass hurricanes. Each place was set with the hotel's white china and a folded white napkin with simple tented place cards perched at the top. Beyond the table and through the glass French doors stood the White House illuminated in the deepening dusk. Past that the Washington Monument glowed from the ring of spotlights below it. During warm weather months, the doors could be opened so guests could stand on the narrow balcony that ran around the rooftop ballroom. I knew that a cold February evening meant the doors would have to stay shut unless guests wanted to wear their coats the entire night.

"The word you're looking for is stark." I rubbed one temple with my fingers. "Are we sure the staff set this for Amelia's rehearsal dinner?"

Kate patted my shoulder. "Look at the bright side. It really puts the focus on the view."

"The bride is going to have a fit," I said, leaving Kate and walking the length of the table. "There's nothing even remotely Valentiney about this room."

"I thought the groom's family had money," Kate said. "You think they could have sprung for a red accent plate at the very least."

"I don't think this is about money." I thought back to the bride's comments about her in-laws. Even though they'd been few and far between, they'd led me to think that the groom's side wasn't crazy about Amelia or her overly themed wedding. If they were trying to balance out the weekend or subtly show their displeasure, this stripped-down dinner would do the trick. "Renting out the Top of the Hay isn't cheap."

"There's nothing we can do about it now. It's not like the groom's side hired us to plan tonight." Kate swept her arms wide. "Not that there was anything to plan."

I shook my head and turned away from the table. "Let's just hope this doesn't make Amelia a mess for tomorrow. The last thing we want is a bride who's spent the entire night before her wedding crying or fuming."

"If we're lucky, Fern gave her champagne while he was getting her ready." Kate pulled her phone out of her hot-pink Kate Spade purse. "I'm going to call him and tell him to put a few Valiums in his bag for tomorrow. Just in case."

I held up a finger. "No more drugging the brides."

Kate shrugged. "Then I'll tell him to bring it for us. If Amelia is in full-blown bridezilla mode, I'd rather be oblivious."

I knew Kate was kidding about taking a Valium, but Fern had

been known to relax his brides with prodigious amounts of bubbly and the occasional crushed-up muscle relaxer. After sending a group of bridesmaids down the aisle who'd all fallen asleep during the ceremony, he'd promised me that he wouldn't do it again.

"We can't do anything about this dinner," I said. "What we need to focus on is finding the sous chef."

"Well, it's Friday night at one of the top hotels in the city. Between the private events and the restaurant, this place will be busy. I'm sure he's working."

"The question is, how do we find out if he attempted to kill his ex-wife without tipping him off?"

"That sounds like a question we should be asking your boyfriend," Kate said. "You did say you were going to tell him what we found out."

I walked out of the ballroom into the foyer that held the elevators and a small coat check area. "You heard me leave him a message."

Kate folded her arms across her chest, exposing even more cleavage than her scoop neck blouse did already. "I heard you leave him a courtesy message. You didn't tell him what we learned. You just asked him to call you back when he got the chance."

"I don't want to be one of those shrewish girlfriends who pesters him while he's at work."

Kate narrowed her eyes at me. "Right. That's what you're worried about. Being high-maintenance."

I let out a breath. "Fine. I didn't want to tell him right away, because I know that once Marcie's ex thinks the police are onto him, he might not be so eager to talk. You and I, on the other hand, might be able to get more genuine reactions by having a casual chat."

"So we're not questioning him, just having a casual chat because we happen to be in the same hotel at the same time?"

I clapped her on the shoulder. "Exactly."

"Don't you think Reese will call this shirting the rules?"

"Skirting the rules?" I continued past the empty coat check

area with its long row of metal hangers. "Not once he realizes that we were already here and just happened to run into him. Now let's check this kitchen. Chances are good they've already started prepping for dinner. If he's not here, we'll check the main catering kitchen on the first floor."

"This feels less like a coincidence and more like a manhunt," Kate mumbled as she followed me through the swinging door and into the kitchen.

Sure enough, a few cooks were standing at the metal tables facing the entrance, and the scent of sautéing onions filled the air. The sounds of chopping stopped as everyone looked up at us.

"Hi," I gave a small wave. "We're the planners for tonight's dinner." A small lie. "We wanted to pop in and introduce ourselves and thank you ahead of time for all your hard work."

A few of the cooks smiled and a few went back to chopping.

"Is Chef Symon working tonight?" I asked.

A lanky man with thinning hair turned around from the industrial stove top. "That's me. I'm Darren Symon. What can I do for you?"

I paused as I kept my smile fixed. I hadn't thought past the part where we found the ex. I really needed to start planning out my interrogations better. "I'm Annabelle and this is Kate. We were here at the Love Brunch the other day, as well."

The chef nodded as if this was information he didn't need. "I hope you enjoyed the food."

"Delicious," Kate said. "The oatmeal soufflé is our favorite."

Chef Symon gave a half snort half laugh. "It's everyone's favorite."

"It was too bad the event was interrupted by the police," I said. "I hope the kitchen wasn't too messed up."

He shrugged. "We're used to it. If it isn't the police, it's a surprise toast by a drunk guest, or an extra-long dance set by the band."

"Tell us about it," Kate said. "We once had a saxophone player do a twenty-minute riff right as we were about to serve the entree."

"You've probably never had a guest taken out of an event to be questioned about a murder before, though," I said, trying to steer the conversation back to Marcie.

His eyes flickered. "I guess not." He motioned to the stove. "I've got to get back to work."

He turned his back to us, and Kate jerked her head toward the door. I knew she was probably right and we should go, but I also knew that we had the element of surprise that the cops wouldn't.

I decided to go for broke. "I'll bet that was a shock, especially when you found out who was being questioned."

Chef Symon stopped stirring and swiveled back around. "Why do you think we'd know anything about who was being questioned?"

"I assumed you'd have heard if your ex-wife was a suspect in a murder investigation," I said. "Then again, she wasn't supposed to be the suspect, was she? She was supposed to be the victim."

All the cooks froze, and their eyes darted between the chef and me. Even Kate held her breath.

Chef Symon blinked slowly a few times. "Marcie was at Love Brunch? She's the reason the police came and disrupted service?" He laughed. "Typical. She's still messing up my life even after we're divorced."

This was not the reaction I'd been expecting. "You didn't know she was here?"

"How would I know? They don't give the guest list to the kitchen, and we never leave the back of the house during an event."

That made sense, I guess. "You're telling me you didn't even know it was her when she made a scene accusing someone else of murdering her assistant?"

"The kitchen is pretty soundproof. The hotel doesn't want guests hearing us banging pans back here." He tilted his head at me. "Did you say her assistant was murdered? Do you mean Marcus?"

"Did you know him?" Kate asked.

An expression clouded his face before disappearing just as quickly. "He and Marcie were old friends from college. I'm really sorry that he's dead. I liked him more than I liked her."

"Did you ever want your ex-wife dead?" I asked.

"I don't know anyone who went thought a divorce that didn't want their ex dead, do you?" he asked in lieu of an answer.

"He makes a good point," Kate whispered.

"I can tell you I never wished any harm on Marcus," he continued. "He always had the best stories about Marcie and the trouble they used to get into. It was always fun to watch her squirm when he blew her perfect princess image out of the water. I'll miss the guy."

"The police don't think he was the intended victim," I said. "They think the killer intended Marcie to die."

The chef raised his eyebrows. "Then it's too bad they failed. I would have liked to buy them a drink." He spun back around. "Now unless you want this dinner to start late, I need to get back to work."

Kate tugged me by the arm until we were standing outside the swinging door. "Well, that was interesting."

"You can say that again. He seemed genuinely surprised to hear about all of it."

"Either he should have a second career as an actor, or he had nothing to do with the murder," Kate said.

I was about to agree with her when a giant potted tree walked past us toward the ballroom, jingling as it went. I exchanged a glance with Kate. "Was that . . .?"

We both followed the jingling plant and watched as Mack lowered the potted palm to the floor. His red, sweaty face brightened when he saw us.

"What are you doing here?" I asked.

"What do you think?" He wiped his hands on his leather pants as he walked over to us. "The bride hired us to come in and upgrade the look. Buster is on his way up with about a thousand pink-and-white balloons to fill the ceiling alcove."

I wondered what the grooms' parents were going to think about the bride hijacking the party they'd planned.

"Finding murder suspects might have just become the least of our worries," Kate said.

I was afraid she was right.

❦ 23 ❦

"Am I through the door yet?" Buster called out from behind a wall of iridescent pink-and-white balloons trying to squeeze through double doors leading into the ballroom. The only indication it was Buster, aside from the deep voice, was the tips of his black leather boots poking out underneath. Otherwise, it was a mass of latex.

Mack rushed forward and tried to push the balloons aside to help Buster through. "Let me help you."

The sound of balloon against balloon and then balloon against leather made Kate put her hands over her ears. Finally Buster and his balloons made it inside, and he let them go to rise up into the recessed alcove that ran down the center of the ceiling. I braced myself for at least one to pop, but none did.

"So how much more decor did Amelia hire you to provide?" I asked. "And since when do you guys do balloons?"

"Normally we'd never touch them," Mack said, looking up at the bobbing sea of pale pink and pearly white orbs above us. "But everyone knows this alcove needs something."

"We've filled it with real flowers, paper flowers, palm fronds, and just greenery before, but Amelia wanted something more fitting for Valentine's Day." Buster tilted his head up and the black motorcycle goggles he wore on his forehead slipped back. "This seemed better than the alternative."

"Which was . . .?" Kate asked.

"Hearts made out of paper doilies and suspended by translucent wire," Mack said. "I put the kibosh on that, let me tell you."

"When did Amelia order all this?" I asked. "We didn't hear a word about it."

Buster's mouth went slack. "You didn't know?" He snapped his head around Mack's. "We assumed you knew."

Mack clamped a hand over his goatee then let it slowly fall away. "We never would have done this if we thought it was behind your back."

I gave a wave of my hand. "Don't worry. It's not your fault. I'm sure Amelia didn't think of it as going behind our backs."

"Brides do this all the time," Kate said, shaking her head. "Since she felt comfortable with you, I'm sure it made sense to add this directly."

I didn't say what I really thought. That Amelia didn't tell us on purpose. She knew we would have advised her against going behind her future mother-in-law's back to change the look of the rehearsal dinner, and like most brides, she didn't want to be told no. I knew in the frenzy of wedding planning it seemed like the best way to get the magazine-worthy weekend Amelia wanted so badly, but once the flowers wilted and the balloons deflated, she would have irate in-laws for years to come. I shrugged to myself. Nothing I could do about it now.

"We still have more trees," Buster said.

Mack shifted from one foot to the other and his leather pants groaned. "And a floral table runner."

I eyed the candles running down the single long table. "Is it low profile?"

Buster crossed his thick arms, and I saw a flash of tattoo beneath the sleeve of his leather jacket. "What do you think?"

"Maybe we should duck out before the families arrive for

dinner," Kate said as Buster and Mack headed out of the ballroom. "Our job is to check on the setup and leave, right? It's not like we have an event timeline to coordinate."

The idea of missing any potential fireworks between Amelia and her mother-in-law was appealing. I also wanted to pop in on Leatrice before it was too late. For once, I was looking forward to telling her about our newest suspects, and I knew hearing about it would perk her up.

"Let's wait until Buster and Mack have finished at least," I said. "Then we can hang out in the lobby to greet the families. That way Amelia and her mother will see that we're here."

Kate gave me a thumbs-up and was about to say something when a look of confusion crossed her face. "What is she doing here?"

I swiveled my head to see Marcie peeking in from the foyer. She spotted us and looked equally startled.

"What are you doing here?" All three of us said simultaneously.

"I thought you had police protection," Kate said, looking around for any trace of cute cops.

"That was just at the office," Marcie said. "And it was only for twenty-four hours. Our building amped up security anyway, so I doubt anyone suspicious is getting in."

"So no one from the wedding industry then," I said.

Marcie laughed as she stepped into the ballroom. "I didn't know they had an event here tonight." Her eyes swept the length of the room. "It looks so different than it did for Love Brunch."

"Buster and Mack went all out for that," I said. "The ballroom is actually pretty classic and simple when it's not carpeted in grass or draped with fabric."

"No toadstools for cocktail tables on a normal day," Kate said.

"I figured that." Marcie smiled. "Even the planters were brought in? I thought the hotel owned those."

"The ones inside the room all belonged to Lush," I said, jerking a thumb toward a nearby palm. "They've brought different ones in for tonight's rehearsal dinner."

"Actually, we're using the big ones from Love Brunch at our wedding tomorrow." Kate dropped her voice in a mock whisper. "Don't tell our bride, but we had Buster and Mack keep them exactly the same since our bride is having a Valentine's Day themed wedding."

"That's smart," Marcie said. "Don't forget to submit it directly to me for publication, and I'll give it special attention."

"That's so nice of you," I said, trying not to betray my excitement.

"I can't wait to see the photos." Marcie glanced over her shoulder then looked at her wrist. "I don't want to keep you though. I'm sure you have lots to do."

Kate exchanged a look with me. "He's in the kitchen."

"What?" Marcie asked, looking behind her again. "What are you talking about?"

Kate rested a hand on the editor's arm. "We know about your ex. He's working up here tonight on our client's party."

Marcie stared at us.

"We already met him," I said. "If you were coming up here to talk to him, I wouldn't recommend it."

Kate shook her head. "He was busy getting ready for tonight and wasn't too happy to talk to us."

"Then you probably figured out that he'd be less excited to talk to me," Marcie said. "It was a mistake to come here."

"I thought your divorce was settled," Kate said. "I don't know about you, but I rarely have the urge to see my exes once things are over. Unless they're not really an ex, and I add them back in the rotation every so often."

I shot Kate a look. The less the editor of *Capital Weddings* knew about my assistant's vibrant love life, the better. "She's joking, but I don't think it will do you any good to reopen old wounds."

"You're right." Marcie ran a hand through her long dark hair. "Of course you're right. I wanted to tell him about Marcus myself since Darren was actually friendly with him, but the last thing I want to do is put your event in jeopardy."

"How could you do that?" Kate asked.

Marcie's face darkened. "Like most chefs, Darren has a temper. If he gets really angry, he might take it out on the food."

I wasn't sure if I believed in chefs imparting moods into their dishes, but I certainly didn't want to take the chance of adding more conflict into the rehearsal dinner.

"I take it your divorce wasn't amicable," I said, even though we'd already heard through the grapevine and from her ex himself that it wasn't.

Marcie gave a mirthless laugh. "You could say that." She bit the edge of her thumbnail. "To be honest, I was coming here to ask him if he was the one who tried to poison me. A part of me thinks he might have murdered Marcus by accident."

"You really believe that?" Kate asked.

"The last time I saw him, he told me he wished I was dead and said to watch my back." Her voice broke. "I didn't take him seriously, and now Marcus is dead because of me."

"You should tell the police," I said, thinking I should do the exact same thing.

Her eyes hardened. "If my gut is right and it's my ex-husband's fault, he's going to need the police all right, but to protect him from me."

❦ 24 ❧

I hesitated before knocking on Leatrice's door. It had been a long day, and I needed a moment to gather myself after fighting Friday night traffic to get home. My shoulders felt like they were in knots, and I had to make a concerted effort to unball my fists. I always got a little tense the night before a wedding, but adding the murder and Leatrice's heart attack on top of it had not helped my overall Zen. I prided myself on being able to stay calm in any crisis, but this was a lot of drama. Even for a wedding planner.

I also needed a second to prepare myself to see Leatrice again. I knew that she'd been cleared to come home, but my mind couldn't help flashing back to seeing my elderly neighbor lying helpless and nearly lifeless on the floor. I closed my eyes and breathed in and out deeply. I let my eyes flutter open and knocked gently on the door, making the frilly paper hearts taped on the wood surface quiver.

Within seconds, Sidney Allen opened it and beamed at me. He waved me inside. "She's been asking about you since we got home."

"I would have come sooner, but we had meetings and then the rehearsal."

"You don't have to explain to me," he said. As an entertainment coordinator, I knew he understood the life of events.

As usual, Sidney Allen wore a dark suit that didn't have much shape and had a wireless headset perched on his head. He touched a finger to the earpiece. "Affirmative. We're on the move."

I glanced around the dim insides of the apartment but didn't see anyone else. A brass floor lamp next to the floral print couch provided the only light, sending a warm glow over the knickknack covered side tables and wooden coffee table strewn with mystery novels and Leatrice's dog-eared private detective manual.

"Are you coordinating an event remotely?" I asked.

He shook his head and the microphone in front of his mouth bobbled. "I'm hooked up to Leatrice in her bedroom. This way she can direct me to find things for her around the apartment without having to raise her voice."

"How clever," I said, thinking how glad I was Richard hadn't discovered this method of bossing people around from a distance.

Sidney Allen led me down the hallway to the bedroom, giving a cursory knock before pushing open the door. "Here we are, love muffin."

Love muffin? Were ridiculous nicknames a new thing with them, or had I really been out of it lately?

"Annabelle." Leatrice sat propped up in bed on what looked like every pillow and cushion in the apartment. Her jet-black hair helmet remained intact--making me wonder if Fern had already been to visit--and although her cheeks were a bit pale, her electric coral lipstick made up for it. She held out her spindly arms and beckoned me forward. "Tell me everything that's been happening."

I gave Sidney Allen a questioning look as I sat down on the bed next to her, not sure if talking about a murder investigation was the best thing to do with a recent heart attack patient. I didn't want to be the one responsible for overexciting her.

"You might as well tell her." He put his hands on his round waist. "If you don't, she'll go drag that police scanner in here and listen to it all night."

Leatrice giggled and squeezed my hands. "My honey bun is such a worrier. I keep telling him I'm fine."

Honey bun? Love muffin? Hoo boy.

"He's right to be concerned, Leatrice. You gave us all quite a scare."

Something flickered across her face, but it was replaced by her wide smile almost instantly. "Nonsense. My little incident had nothing to do with your murder case or with my scanner. I wasn't even listening to it then."

"What *were* you doing?" In all the chaos, I'd never asked how or why Leatrice had nearly died.

Her eyes went to Sidney Allen and her cheeks colored. "A little too much romance I'm afraid."

I braced myself for a potentially traumatizing overshare. "That's okay. You don't need to--"

"We were dancing," Sidney Allen said. "I was teaching her the tango."

I let out a breath. "Dancing?" I tried to imagine the egg-shaped man dancing the tango.

"The tango is a very sensual dance," Leatrice said with a wink, "and very vigorous."

I tried to remove both of those words from my brain as I thought of Leatrice and Sidney Allen. "I'm just glad you're okay."

"I'm fine." She gave my hands a shake. "But enough about me. There's nothing interesting to say about a hospital visit. I can tell you the food was dreadful, but the waitresses were lovely."

I didn't remind her that they were orderlies, not waitresses.

Sidney Allen slipped out of the room, and Leatrice lowered her voice. "What's going on with the case?"

I thought back to what Leatrice knew so far. "You remember the redhead from the magazine who told us about Marcie's broken office door and the dead roses? Well, she's been having an affair with the photographer Maxwell Gray."

"Don't I know that name?"

I nodded. "He's been loosely connected to a few of our cases before. Oh, and someone was killed in his new studio during a party."

"Is he connected to this case?"

"He conspired with Cassandra--that's the redhead--to spook Marcie with the dead flowers so she'd quit. The plan was Cassandra would get Marcie's job, and Maxwell would get back on the 'Best Of' list he'd been kicked off." I took a breath. "They claim they didn't have anything to do with the broken lock or the poisoned chocolates though."

Leatrice looked like Christmas had come early. "Two new suspects. How exciting!"

"I forgot Marcie's hairdresser, who was also upset not to be on the list, and her ex-husband. That makes four."

"My detective manual says the spouse should always be looked at very carefully." She steepled her fingers and drummed them against each other. "Did he have a good reason to want her dead?"

"Their divorce wasn't friendly," I said. "He was paying a lot of alimony, at least that's what we heard. He claims he didn't kill him, but Kate and I didn't expect him to confess."

Her fingers froze. "You tracked him down?"

"Not exactly. He's a chef at the hotel where our clients are holding their rehearsal dinner tonight. We just happened to be going there."

Leatrice drew in her breath sharply. "One of your suspects is a chef? That would have made it easy for him to tamper with the chocolates, wouldn't it?"

"Possibly," I said, "but we have no idea how he could have gotten his hands on them. As far as we know, he wasn't anywhere near the magazine offices, and everyone swears the box of chocolates never left the editor's desk. I'm sure Marcie would have noticed her ex-husband lurking around."

"What about the planner who hates you and was at the magazine when Richard dropped off his truffles?" Leatrice asked. "She had motive and opportunity."

"Brianna? Reese questioned her but doesn't think she did it." I didn't add that I thought my boyfriend was being snowed by her innocent Southern belle act. "Unfortunately, she blames us for being added to the suspect list."

"Oh dear." Leatrice frowned. "Did I get you in hot water with one of your colleagues?"

I patted Leatrice's wrinkled hand. "There was no love lost between us to begin with. I wouldn't worry about it."

Leatrice rearranged herself on the collection of pillows and couch cushions. "So what's our next move?"

"I have a big wedding tomorrow, and you need to stay in bed, so I don't think either of us have a next move. Plus, Reese will have me put in protective custody if I don't butt out."

Leatrice took my hands again. "I hope you'll tell him to stop by. He's such a nice young man, Annabelle."

"Look who's here," Sidney Allen called as he walked back into the room.

"I would have been here sooner, sweetie," Fern said, bustling into the room with a bag over each arm. "I was just now able to pull myself away from the bride."

"Amelia kept you busy until now?" I asked. "The dinner should have been in full swing."

Fern held up both palms. "Do. Not. Ask. The bride wanted to change looks between the church and the hotel. We're going to be out of hairstyles by the time the wedding rolls around. Don't blame me if I have to send her down the aisle with a Mohawk tomorrow."

He set the bags on the end of the bed and gave Leatrice the once-over. "You look a thousand times better already. All we need is to spruce up your look with some color. How do feel about a smoky eye?"

"It's nighttime," I said.

Fern looked at me as if I were a simpleton. "Which is the best time for a smoky eye." He produced a handful of nail polish bottles and held them out for Leatrice to inspect. "What do you think about silver glitter for your toes?"

"Do you have anything more Valentiney?" she asked, giving Sidney Allen a suggestive smile. "Maybe a sexy red?"

I was glad Richard was not here to see this. He might have regretted giving her CPR.

Fern dug in one of his bags and produced a bottle of fire engine red polish. "What about this? We could always do a clear glitter top coat for some sparkle."

Leatrice clapped her hands. "Perfect." She blew a kiss to Sidney Allen. "What do you think, sweetie pie?"

"You'd look beautiful in any color, cupcake," he said, blowing her a kiss back.

That was my cue to leave. Between the sweetie pies, cupcakes, honey buns, and love muffins, I was getting both hungry and nauseated.

"I'll leave you and Fern to your makeover." I stood and started backing toward the door. "I still need to go over the schedule for tomorrow and check my emergency kit."

"You'll keep me posted about the case, won't you?" Leatrice asked as Fern unpacked his pedicure supplies on the bed.

"I promise you nothing will happen between now and the next time I see you," I said. "But I'll make sure Reese keeps you updated if he finds out anything new. And I'll see you tomorrow morning, Fern."

Fern gave me a finger wave over his shoulder, his enormous topaz ring flashing at me. "Bright and early."

Sidney Allen led me to the front door. "Your visit really perked her up."

"Then by the time Fern's done with her, she's going to be on the ceiling," I said. "Just make sure she gets some rest."

He told me he would as he closed the door behind me. I started up the stairs to my apartment, pausing when I heard the building's front door open.

"Hey, babe." Reese smiled as he walked in, but I noticed that he looked as tired as I felt. His white button-down was wrinkled and had some sort of stain on the collar with the sleeves rolled up to his elbows.

I waited for him on the landing and let him pull me into a hug. His arms felt good wrapped around me, and I felt the familiar flutter of butterflies as I pressed a hand against his hard chest muscles.

"I was visiting Leatrice," I said, indicating her door with my head.

"Should I pop in and say hi?" he asked.

"Fern's giving her a pedicure right now, so she may be a bit distracted. Better to wait until tomorrow. The rest of us will be working all day, even Sidney Allen, so it would be a good time to visit her."

"Consider it done." Reese slipped an arm around my waist as we headed up to our apartment. "Are you ready for your wedding?"

"I'd better be," I said. "I just hope the photographer doesn't play the diva card."

"You're used to divas though. Do I need to remind you about Richard?"

"True," I said. "But I may have ticked this one off by accusing him of trying to kill Marcie."

Reese stopped mid-step and shook his head slowly. "Do I want to know?"

I explained our visit to Maxwell, the encounter with Cassandra, discovering Marcie's ex-husband was a chef at The Hay-Adams, and talking to him at the hotel. When I closed with explaining Marcie's theory that her ex was behind Marcus's death, Reese gaped at me.

"I honestly don't know how you get all your wedding work done with the amount of sleuthing you do."

I smiled up at him. "Impressed?"

He ran a hand through his hair. "That's not the word that comes to mind."

"Most of the information fell into our laps," I said. "And it was a coincidence that Marcie's ex happened to work at the hotel we were going to anyway. The good news is now you can run with all the clues we discovered. It's not like I'll have time to do any investigating tomorrow during my wedding."

Reese mumbled something about small favors as we reached our apartment door.

"You brought up one good point," I said as Reese jiggled the key in the lock. "I haven't heard from Richard at all today. It's not like him to go radio silent like this."

He pushed open the door, but neither of us went inside. It both sounded and smelled like someone was cooking in our kitchen.

"There you are," Richard rushed to the door in a white chef's hat with Hermes poking out of the pocket of a matching apron. "I've been waiting forever. I have so much to tell you two."

25

Reese closed the door behind us. He hadn't said a word since we'd walked in on Richard, and I couldn't tell if he was in shock or contemplating how fast it would take him to move out.

"When did you get here?" I asked, even though it was only one of about a hundred questions I had for him.

Richard glanced at his Gucci watch. "A couple of hours by now." He pointed a wooden spoon at me. "I expected you to be home much earlier. I thought rehearsals were usually around five o'clock."

"They are, but Kate and I checked in on the rehearsal dinner at the Top of the Hay, and then I stopped in to see Leatrice."

Richard spun on his heel and headed back to the kitchen. "How is the old thing?"

"She looks almost like her usual self," I said. "The heart attack didn't put much of a damper on her energy."

"That's too bad," Richard said. "I suppose it was too much to hope she'd take up crocheting instead of playing neighborhood spy."

Despite his complaints, I knew Richard had a soft spot for Leatrice. Not that he would ever admit it.

Reese dropped his worn satchel on the floor next to the couch. "At least we don't have to order pizza tonight."

Richard gasped and poked his head over the counter dividing the kitchen and living room. "Have you been serving this man nothing but pizza?"

"No." I heard the defensive tone in my voice, and I dropped it to a mumble. "We also order Chinese."

Reese pulled me down with him onto the couch. "It's okay." He nuzzled my neck. "I like pizza." He glanced over his shoulder. "I also like privacy."

Hermes scampered out from the kitchen and jumped onto the couch next to us, running from one end to the other and walking across our laps in the process.

"Sorry about this," I whispered. "Maybe we should change the locks."

"Doesn't Leatrice have one of those key-making molds? How long until she cloned our new key and made copies for everyone?"

"About a week," I admitted, closing my eyes and wishing I could kick Richard out as Reese nibbled my neck. I felt Hermes circle a few times before curling up next to me.

"I hope you're in the mood for steak, Detective." Richard called out over the sound of something sizzling in a pan. "I'm searing it in herb butter. Nothing fancy."

Reese moaned a little, and my own stomach rumbled. I pulled back and swatted at him. "Are you moaning because of me or the steak?"

He gave me a crooked grin, his hazel eyes deepening to green. "A little of both." He laughed as I swatted him a second time. "Hey, I didn't eat lunch."

Richard cleared his throat. "Don't you want to know what I found out about our victim?"

"Is there anyone who *isn't* investigating my murder case?" Reese asked.

"Why are you checking out Marcus?" I asked Richard. "I thought you already knew him. Didn't you hire him to work for Richard Gerard Catering?"

"Yes, but to be honest, I didn't do my due diligence. This was back when we were so busy I couldn't think straight, so I was in too much of a rush to check out the candidates like I should have."

"Did Marcus give references?" I asked.

"Oh, I called those and they all said nice things about him, but who gives a reference who won't say nice things about you? I should have checked out the details on his resume, and that's what I did today."

I sat up straighter. "Are you saying Marcus put things on his resume that weren't true?"

"He stretched the truth," Richard said. "For one, he claimed to be a college graduate, but he wasn't."

"I know he went to college." I dropped my shoes on the floor and tucked my legs up under me. "He and Marcie went to the same school."

"He went," Richard said. "He didn't finish. I called the university today and apparently Marcus was expelled."

Now Reese straightened. "Expelled? Why?"

"He was arrested." Richard paused for what I was sure was dramatic effect. "In his senior year he stole a campus police car and went joyriding. They caught him and he was arrested for DUI and kicked out. He never graduated even though he only had a few weeks left to go."

"I almost feel sorry for him," I said. "A lot of people do dumb things in college, but not everyone gets kicked out and loses the chance to get a degree."

"Feel more sorry he got poisoned," Reese said under his breath.

"Do you want to know the kicker?" Richard asked. "Stealing a police car is a felony, so even though Marcus only got probation and time served, he was a convicted felon."

"Doesn't that make it harder to get a job?" I asked.

Richard pointed his wooden spoon at me through the divider.

"Bingo. You're supposed to tell your employers or at least check the box on the job application form, but we don't use a form to hire people so it never came up."

"I'd never think to ask an applicant if they'd been convicted of a felony," I said. "Not in the wedding world at least."

"Who knows?" Reese cocked an eyebrow. "Your industry could be littered with convicted felons."

"That would actually explain a lot."

"It explains why Marcus had to hit up his old friend for a job at *Capital Weddings,*" Richard continued. "Especially if other employers were more thorough in their background checks. It also proves that my instincts about him were right on the money. At least after the first week."

I didn't remind him that he'd only fired Marcus after discovering that the man had been sending out proposals laden with profanity. I'd learned that perfect recall was not a trait Richard always valued.

Richard appeared from the kitchen holding two plates with oven mitts. He set them down on the dining room table, which I noticed for the first time was set with both silverware and glasses, then returned to the kitchen.

"So our unintended victim wasn't as squeaky clean as we thought," Reese said as he stood. "I'm not sure that brings us any closer to figuring out why someone wanted to kill his boss."

"Maybe not." Richard reappeared with a third plate. "It was more for my own illumination. I always felt there was more to Marcus than met the eye."

"That reminds me," I said as I sat in the chair Reese pulled out for me. "What did you find out about the coroner's report that made you rush off last night?"

"How did you know it was about the coroner's report?" Reese asked as he took the seat next to mine.

"Kate may have overheard you while she was hunting down a vending machine," I said, inhaling the scent of the steak and grilled vegetables from the plate in front of me.

"I suppose it won't hurt to tell you." Reese cut a piece from his filet mignon. "The final coroner's report showed more in the victim's stomach than one chocolate."

"So the original report was wrong? Marcus ate more than the chocolate?" I nearly dropped the fork I'd picked up. "That's great. That means it could have been something other than Richard's truffles."

Reese held up a finger. "Not more than chocolate. More than one chocolate."

"I don't get it," Richard said. "Didn't all the witnesses say he only ate the cherry liquor?"

Reese took a bite and chewed it slowly. "According to the coroner, he ate more than one. Quite a few more."

"That means the people at the magazine who said he ate just one were lying." I put my fork down. "That means Cassandra was lying. But why?"

"Who's Cassandra?" Richard asked.

"Someone who had a motive to kill Marcie and plenty of opportunity," I told him. "And someone who's already lied to us more than once."

Reese took a sip of his wine. "So much for my day off. Looks like I'll be paying a visit to this Cassandra."

❦ 26 ❦

"**T**hese trees look familiar," Kate said as we stepped into the ballroom at The Wharf Intercontinental the next day.

The tall trees in planters lined against the wall were hung with strands of pink orchids, although I suspected they weren't the same orchids from the Love Brunch even though they were nearly the same color. I reached into my dress pocket for my phone so I could snap some photos of the setup before I got too busy and forgot.

"We kept the translucent wire and changed out the flowers," Mack said, coming in behind us. "Amelia wanted more of a blush tone anyway."

"How is our Valentine's bride?" Buster asked, staggering past us with a massive arrangement comprised entirely of red-and-pink roses.

"We just came from upstairs," I said. "Fern's keeping her and the bridesmaids happy."

Buster centered the towering centerpiece on one of the tables designed to look like a giant X and draped with red silk linens. "Are we sure this doesn't look more bordello than wedding?"

Considering the amount of red being used in the wedding, it was a fair question. I took a quick picture of the roses and studied it on my phone screen as Kate looked over my shoulder.

"The pink softens it." Kate shook a few gummy bears into her hand and passed the mini cellophane bag to me. "Otherwise this would be more red-light district than Valentine's Day."

"The cupid flower girls don't scream bordello," I said, popping a couple of the sweet squishy candies into my mouth and passing the packet to Mack. "They're adorable in their white dresses, feather wings, and bows and arrows."

"Only because we talked the bride out of having her brides-maids dressed like cupids," Kate reminded me. "That would have been less adorable and more 'leave the money on the nightstand.'"

I elbowed her. "Do I need to remind you the bride wants to get this wedding published in a magazine?"

"As soon as we get the pink lighting in, it won't look so intense," Mack said, handing the gummy bears back to Kate after Buster declined them. "What time does John Farr Lighting load in?"

I glanced at the time on my phone. "Now." The sugar from the candy gave me a needed boost, and I felt glad Kate always carried a stash in her dress. "I should also check on Sidney Allen. He's coordinating the confetti cannons and the dove release."

"Is Leatrice home alone?" Mack asked.

"Reese is going to visit her," I said. "And I know Sidney Allen plans to duck out the second those doves fly around in their heart formation and get back into their cage."

Mack pressed his brows together. "Why don't I have Prue stay with her? She was going to take Merry out for a walk around Georgetown anyway."

"Good idea," Buster said.

A head poked into the room, and I recognized our banquet captain for the evening, Luis.

"The haiku poet is asking where you'd like him to set up," Luis said, his face telling me how odd he found the concept of a haiku poet at a wedding.

I turned to Kate. "Let's go handle the Haiku Crew."

We left Buster and Mack in the ballroom and followed Luis to where a couple stood, each holding a battered case I knew contained their vintage typewriters.

"The cocktail hour will be in here," I said, leading them into a smaller ballroom with walls we'd draped in ivory fabric.

Kate pointed to the rustic wooden table flanked by old-fashioned red-tufted sofas. "Does that setup work for you?"

The pair thanked us and began unpacking their typewriters and stacks of paper onto the desk. I motioned to another table across the room. "That's the station for the paper cutter who'll be making Valentine's cards on the fly."

Luis nodded. "Did I read the BEO right, and is there really going to be a life-sized chocolate fountain?"

The BEO, or banquet event order, told the hotel crew every detail about the party so they could set up the rooms accordingly and so the kitchen could time the food. Chances were good that the words "life-sized chocolate fountain" had never appeared on one before.

"Yes," I said, "but the company promised me they cover the carpet with a plastic tray. Like the ones used for ice sculptures."

Luis scratched his head. "That's got to be a big tray." He didn't look convinced about the plan. To be honest, neither was I.

Kate and I returned to the foyer. I pulled my wedding day timeline from my pocket and scanned the first page. "We're on schedule. Ahead even."

"Good." Kate walked me over to a cocktail table. "We have a few minutes for me to tell you about happy hour last night."

I sat and flattened out my folded schedule on the table, checking off "haiku poets arrive" and feeling a certain satisfaction that setup was going smoothly. "How can you drink the night before a wedding?"

She waved away my concerns. "I only had one drink and I nursed it. The important point is that Cassandra joined us."

"You were socializing with one of our murder suspects? What about the information Reese learned from the coroner?" I asked. "Cassandra is the one who told us Marcus only ate one truffle, and now we know that wasn't true. She could be lying about everything, including the fact that she killed him."

Kate flicked a hand through her hair. "I didn't know that then, did I? Besides, I still can't imagine her killing someone. If she wanted to kill Marcie, wouldn't she have said something when Marcus chowed down on the poison?"

She made a good point. It would take a seriously hard-hearted person to watch an innocent man eat something you knew would kill him. "I guess so. Marcie was the person she wanted to get rid of."

"I'm not even sure she really wanted to get rid of Marcie either," Kate said, crossing her leg. "After a couple of drinks, she was crying about the whole thing. She feels guilty about getting involved with Maxwell and sending the dead flowers to her boss."

"She's probably scared we're going to tell and she'll get fired."

Kate shook her head. "I don't think so. She seemed broken up about the whole thing. I get the feeling she got pulled into it by Maxwell sweet-talking her, but I don't even know if she wanted to be the head editor. She probably liked the sound of it, especially the way Maxwell sold it to her."

I cringed. "I still can't believe someone as young as her was attracted to a man who could be her grandfather. The dating scene in DC can't be that bad."

"Before Reese, how many dates had you had?" Kate asked.

I thought for a moment. "Okay, fine. You made your point. I still say anyone desperate enough to sleep with Maxwell Gray is desperate enough to commit murder. Plus, since she works at the magazine, she had opportunity that no other suspect had. The killer had to have access to the chocolates after Richard delivered them."

"Brianna had access. Richard saw her at the magazine offices when he delivered the box, and we have no idea how long she stayed after he left."

I tapped my pen on my schedule. "You know I'd love it to be her, but how was she supposed to know there would be chocolates to poison? The killer had to have the poison on them to inject into the truffles. I think Brianna is a nasty piece of work, but it seems odd that she'd be walking around with nicotine poisoning on her."

"Then Marcie's chef ex-husband," Kate said. "He could have done it. He's a smoker."

"How do you know that?" I thought back to our talk with Chef Symon. Had he mentioned smoking?

Kate held up a hand and wiggled her fingers. "The tips of his fingers were stained and so were his teeth. I wouldn't be surprised if he smoked a pack or two a day."

"Good eyes, Kate."

"I've gotten good at spotting the signs. You know I don't date smokers, and some of them try to hide it." She made a face. "I can always know for sure by the first kiss, but who wants to waste an hour or two?"

I didn't point out that some people waited more than an hour before a first kiss. Reese and I had taken months to get to that point, but I knew Kate found our romance to be glacially slow.

"Even if Marcie's ex smokes a lot, that doesn't mean he used nicotine to try to kill her," I said. "If he was smart, he'd want to use something that directed suspicion away from him. If his smoking habit was common knowledge, I doubt he'd use that as his murder weapon."

Kate frowned at me. "So we're back to Cassandra?"

"Looks like it."

"I'm telling you, she was broken up about Marcus last night. Apparently they'd become pretty good friends, even though he was also tight with Marcie. Cassandra knew all about Marcie's divorce, and I know her boss didn't share all that dirt with her."

"So Marcus went out with the staff and dished on their boss and his old friend?" I eyed Kate. "That doesn't seem cool."

"I got the feeling from Cassandra that Marcus was the type of person who was a ton of fun to hang out with, but you wouldn't trust him as far as you could throw him." She put a hand to her chest. "Personally, I'd never dream of revealing your dirty secrets. Mostly because you have none, but the second you do, Annabelle, they're safe with me."

"That's very comforting. Do you think Marcus knew dirt on Cassandra? Maybe she told him about Maxwell and the scheme to scare Marcie out of her job."

Kate drummed her polished nails on the table. "She was pretty loose-lipped last night. If she was always that chatty after a couple of drinks, she could have let it slip."

"I wonder," I said, rolling an idea round in my mind. "What if Cassandra's victim wasn't Marcie? What if it was Marcus all along?"

Kate sat up and uncrossed her legs. "You think we've been looking at the wrong victim?"

"I'm just saying that she definitely had a motive to kill him if there was a chance he'd spill her secrets. Not only would Cassandra have gotten fired if anyone found out, chances are good the scandal would have been so bad she never would have gotten another job in this town."

"That's true. She would have been ruined."

"We've already established that she had the most opportunity," I said. "Maybe we were right about that but wrong about the motive. Her motive to kill Marcus would have been much stronger if she was afraid he'd reveal what she'd done."

"So she poisoned chocolates meant for Marcie because she knew her boss wouldn't eat them?" Kate asked.

"She told us she knew Marcie was on a diet. Plus, if she knew which truffles were poisoned, she could even eat one herself to throw us off the trail."

"That's clever," Kate said. "So what do we do about it?"

I pulled my phone out of my dress pocket. "Reese was going to talk to her today. Now he'll have a few more questions to ask her."

Kate grabbed my arm. "What if he's questioning her right now? He doesn't know she was actually trying to kill Marcus and not Marcie."

"At least we think she was," I said, pressing speed dial for my boyfriend and hearing it go to voice mail. "There's always the possibility we're wrong. It wouldn't be the first time."

I left him a message, hoping he'd get it in time.

Kate squinted at something over my shoulder. "Is there anything in the meeting room across the hall?"

I followed her line of sight. "Just the candy we had the bellman deliver for us when we arrived."

Kate stood quickly. "The candy for the display later tonight? That's the vendor room?"

"Didn't I tell you the hotel catering exec needed to move us to that room?" I asked. "Why?"

Kate started speed walking toward the doors. "I'm pretty sure I just saw Brianna poke her head out of there."

✽ 27 ✽

"**Y**ou must be seeing things," I said as we walked down the hotel corridor toward the bride's suite. "There was no trace of anyone in that room, and the candy boxes were all there."

"If I'm hallucinating visions of Brianna, I think I need to see a doctor."

I patted her arm. "It's been a long week."

Kate pushed the door open since it stood slightly ajar. We'd thrown the dead bolt earlier so it would prevent the door from closing all the way and to keep us from having to knock every time we popped in and out of the room.

I followed Kate inside and took a moment. The suite was a very different scene than it had been the day before. Duffel bags littered the floor, their contents spilling out of them, and garment bags hung across the backs of chairs and from the tops of doors. A decimated tray of bagels and muffins sat on a room service trolley, and a couple of empty bottles of bubbly surrounded by glass flutes were on the coffee table.

The air held the scent of hair spray and coffee, and I noticed a couple of cardboard drink holders jammed into a nearby trash can.

It was hard to hear much over the pulsating hip-hop music, but the muffled sound of female voices came from the direction of the bathroom. As Kate and I walked closer, I could hear the distinct sound of Fern's voice rising above all the others.

"I'm telling you girls, the last thing you want to deal with on your wedding night is a big--"

"How's it going in here?" I asked, drowning out whatever inappropriate advice Fern had been dispensing.

Fern stood at the mirror behind the bride, who was perched on a padded stool. He held a curling iron in one hand and a can of hair spray in the other. His hot-pink pants looked impossibly snug and matched his spread-collared shirt. Instead of his usual topaz ring, a pink heart-shaped stone that looked big enough to be a ring pop glittered on his finger. "Fabulous. We've changed up the hair on the bridesmaids a little bit."

"Inspired by Valentine's Day, naturally," Amelia added, not moving her head but waving at us in the reflection.

I glanced at the other women in the room and tried not to let my face show my surprise.

"They've got feathered bangs," Kate whispered to me through a plastered-on smile.

"I can see that." I didn't let my expression falter as I looked at the collection of Farrah Fawcett winged hairdos surrounding us.

"They're wings," one of the woman said, rolling her eyes. "Get it? Cupid? Wings?"

I got it, and I was going to kill Fern. How were we supposed to submit the wedding to magazines when all the bridesmaids looked like they'd escaped from the eighties?

"Did you cut their hair?" I asked, trying to keep the panic out of my voice.

Fern winked at me. "Just a teensy snip here and there. Nothing that won't grow out."

Amelia was going to owe her bridesmaids big time, I thought as I took in the facial expressions of the women in the room. If they ever spoke to her again.

"Are you giving the bride feathered hair too?" Kate asked.

Fern shook his head and his tidy man bun bobbled on the top of his head. "We're sticking to an updo for Amelia, but I'm curling the two sides of the bun together into the center to make a heart. Isn't that going to be darling?"

I fought the urge to slap my forehead and then Fern's. "Are you sure about this, Amelia? You're going to have these photos for the rest of your life. Don't you want to stick with something timeless like the French twist you did at the trial?"

She reached for a rocks glass filled with what looked like slightly pink milk and swirled the ice cubes in the bottom. "Fern told me I should stand out on my wedding day."

I shot Fern a look then smiled at Amelia. "You're the bride. You're the only one wearing a big white dress. You're carrying a red bouquet of roses shaped like a heart. Trust me, you already stand out."

"I'm surprised you all aren't drinking bubbly," Kate said, assessing the tumblers of blush-pink milk the bridesmaids held.

"I brought something better." Fern produced a pink-and-red bottle from behind a row of styling products on the counter. "Bailey's Strawberries and Cream. So sweet you don't know you're drinking booze. Mix it with a little vodka and it's even better."

Perfect. Served me right for leaving Fern unattended with the bridal party for too long. I should have been glad Amelia didn't have a Mohawk.

"May I see you outside for a moment?" I asked Fern through gritted teeth.

He topped off his own glass of Bailey's and tossed it back before answering. "Of course, sweetie." He gave Amelia's shoulder a squeeze. "I'll be right back to tell you girls my secret for the longest--"

I pulled him out by the elbow before he could finish his sentence and marched him into the living room. "What on earth are you doing in there?"

He smoothed his shirt after I released him. "Keeping Miss

Nervous Nelly from having a panic attack and deciding she wants to rent flying monkeys and dress them in wings for the reception. What do you think I'm doing?"

"It looks like you're getting them drunk and making them look like members of an eighties hair band," Kate said.

Fern giggled. "That's just the happy by-product. What? You don't like the feathers?"

"It's a little much," I said. "I was hoping the bridal party could be the one normal element of the wedding."

"Then perhaps you should have mentioned that before I used three cans of hair spray to get those bangs to stay put." He sniffed and folded his arms over his chest. "If you want me to do boring old updos, I suppose I can redo everything."

"Thank you," I said, letting out a breath. "And if you make the bride look like an extra from *Star Wars* with some crazy sculpted heart on the top of her head, I'll tell everyone you shop at outlet stores."

He sucked in air. "You wouldn't."

I cocked an eyebrow at him and remained silent.

"Fine." He threw his hands over his head. "You win. Boring hair." He held up his pointer finger. "But I get to add spray glitter after the ceremony."

I extended my hand. "Deal. As long as the glitter isn't red."

We shook on it, and he flounced back into the bathroom muttering about needing more booze and hair spray. I heard him begin to regale the bridesmaids with his patented technique for doing something that involved whipped cream, and I walked away before I heard any details that might scar me for life.

Kate pulled out her phone and glanced at the screen. "The lighting is in. John Farr's asking if we want to check it out."

"Let's go." I felt my own phone buzz and slipped it out of my pocket. Richard's name flashed on the screen.

"My life is torture," he said when I answered.

"What are you going on about? I know you don't have an event today."

"That's what's so torturous." He sighed. "I have no legitimate reason not to stay here with Leatrice all day."

"You're with her right now?" I followed Kate out of the suite. "Buster and Mack sent Prue over with baby Merry. That's going to be a full house in a few minutes."

"The baby's coming?" Richard's voice trembled.

"She's a baby, Richard. You can't be afraid of a baby. You used to feel the same way about dogs, remember?" I said. "Then you got Hermes and changed your mind."

"Hermes is unique," Richard said. "It's not every dog who can tell the difference between wool and cashmere."

And it wasn't every dog that wore a designer cashmere sweater. I'd long suspected that the dog's preferences were more Richard's than anything else.

"I'm sure Leatrice appreciates you bringing Hermes to see her," I said.

"Those two are as thick as thieves," Richard muttered, not sounding happy about it. "They're watching a Matlock rerun and eating popcorn."

As the little Yorkie's sometimes babysitter, Leatrice had formed a special bond with the dog and often treated him like a girlfriend. The two had gone to the movies, gone out for ice cream, and she'd once even given them matching manicures. Richard tolerated it because he hated the idea of putting Hermes in a kennel when he worked and had yet to find a dog sitter who would spoil the creature like Leatrice would.

"And what are you doing?" I asked as Kate and I stepped into the elevator.

"Plotting my escape. As soon as Prue arrives, I'm out of here. A baby and a dog should be enough to keep the old girl amused."

"Remember what you told me about Marcus last night?" I asked him but didn't wait for an answer. "Kate also found out that Marcus had a reputation for being indiscreet with people's secrets. We think he may have known all about Cassandra and Maxwell and their plot to scare Marcie into quitting."

"And you think they decided to poison Marcie before Marcus told her?" His voice crackled as the elevator took us to the ball-room level.

"We think Marcus was the intended victim all along," Kate said loudly, leaning in to the phone.

"Really?" He sounded intrigued.

"We assumed the killer was after Marcie because the chocolates were intended for her, but Cassandra knew she was on a diet and knew how close her boss was to Marcus. It wouldn't be a stretch to think she'd give the truffles to him."

"You might be right, Annabelle. She did work in the office, after all, and had access to the box as soon as I delivered it. Have you told all this to Reese?"

"I left him a message. Hopefully he gets it before he interviews her."

The elevator doors pinged open and we stepped out. The foyer had gone through a transformation since we'd left. Crimson silk cloths draped high-top tables, and panels of white fabric now covered the walls with LED spotlights on the floor, giving them a pink glow.

"Whoa," Kate said. "I'm almost afraid to look inside the ballrooms."

"Let's see how the X and O tables look."

"X and O?" Richard asked.

"The guest tables are shaped like giant Xs and Os," I explained. "You know, like you sign a letter? Hugs and kisses?"

"Darling, have you ever known me to sign a letter with Xs and Os?"

He had a point. "Not you, but people do it. Our bride does it in every email she's sent us for the past year. It's her signature closing. Since it fits with Valentine's Day, Buster and Mack have designed the guest tables to be Xs and Os."

"This I have to see."

I heard voices in the background followed by a series of yips and some baby babble. "What do you mean? Are you coming here? Now?"

Kate stared at me and made wild waving motions with her hands. The last thing we needed in an already overly dramatic day was Richard.

"If you think I'm spending the day with a teenager, a baby, a dog, and an old lady, you're out of your mind. I'll be there in ten minutes."

"Wait--" I said before I heard nothing but dial tone. I looked down at my phone then up at Kate. "The good news is he isn't bringing the dog."

We walked to a cocktail table and took out our schedules, checking a few items off the list. Kate took a call on her cell and made another check mark on her timeline.

"The chocolate fountain people are at the loading dock," she said, tapping her pen on the paper. "You know, the more I think about it, the more I think I'd rather have the dog. At least we could dress him like a cherub and send him down the aisle with the flower girls. We can't do that with Richard. Now, Fern maybe."

"Whatever you do," I said, clutching her hands, "don't give Fern any ideas."

Her eyes caught something over my shoulder and her mouth fell open. "Too late."

❧ 28 ❦

"**Y**ou can't be serious," I told Fern as the long red velvet cape swirled around his ankles, a black-and-white diamond-patterned cummerbund cinching his waist.

"I'm the King of Hearts," he said, "and I think the look is very subtle."

"Is your cape lined in leopard-print fur?" Kate asked, reaching out and touching the edge of it.

"It's faux, sweetie, but yes." He spun for us and the cape belled out around him. "I got this specially for sending the bride down the aisle. I even have a scepter to poke those hussies with if they don't stay in line."

I put two fingers to my temple and made small circles with them. The wedding was teetering on the edge of kitsch as it was. Having a hairdresser direct the processional with a pretend scepter would easily send it skittering into comic territory.

"No scepters," I said.

Fern's face fell. "First no feathered hair and now no scepters? I hope this isn't going to be another basic wedding, Annabelle."

"I would love a basic wedding where the dog ring bearers don't run off with the rings, a groomsman doesn't accidentally moon the congregation when his suspenders snap, and the shuttles don't take the guests to the wrong hotel," I said, waving my hands in the air. "If you can get me one of those, I'd be deliriously happy."

Fern's eyes widened at my outburst. "If that's what you want, fine, but it sounds boring to me." He gave a small shrug. "If it really bothers you, I won't use the scepter."

"Thank you," I said. "Now how close is the bridal party to being ready and unfeathered?"

"They're putting on the dresses now," Fern said. "All I need to do is attach the wings to the flower girls, and I can bring them down."

I flipped to the ceremony page of my timeline, checking the time on my sheet with the clock on the wall. "Then we're right on time. I owe you one." I held up a hand before he could speak. "But I'm still not going along with the scepter."

He mumbled something about me being no fun during murder investigations as he spun and walked back toward the elevator bank.

"Does this have anything to do with the case?" Kate asked once Fern's swirling red cape had vanished behind the closing elevator doors.

I waited until a lighting technician passed carrying a ladder. "You mean am I a little tense knowing that one of our vendors today is a possible accessory to murder? Maybe."

"Maxwell?" Kate glanced around us. "I thought we decided he didn't kill anyone."

"I don't think he did, but if we're right about Cassandra, then he was part of the reason she killed Marcus. Who's to say he didn't suggest she bump off Mr. Loose Lips?"

"You said Reese was going to talk to her today, right?" Kate gnawed the edge of her bottom lip. "If Cassandra implicates Maxwell, you don't think your boyfriend would arrest him in the middle of our wedding, do you?"

My stomach clenched. That hadn't occurred to me. "He wouldn't dare," I said, sounding more confident than I felt.

"Even so," Kate said. "I'm going to find Maxwell and make sure he takes all our detail shots before he gets hauled off to the pig house."

I scratched my head for a moment as I tried to decipher her words. "Do you mean the big house, like prison?"

"Big house?" Kate's brows furrowed together. "I thought it was called the pig house."

"Nope."

She shrugged. "Too bad. Pig house sounds much better."

As she hurried off to find Maxwell, I took another peek at my timeline. Time for me to see if Buster and Mack had set out the escort card display. I knew their plan had been to assemble it inside the ballroom before walking it to the foyer right before guests arrived.

I pulled open one side of the heavy ballroom doors and ducked inside. The room had completely transformed since Kate and I had left. Flowers covered each of the large X tables, which we'd made using several long rectangles, and massive arrangements hung from the ceiling over each of the Os, which had been created by connecting multiple serpentine tables to form an oval-shaped table with a hole in the center. The X tables held one towering arrangement of pink-and-red roses, while the Os had a low runner of roses and hydrangea that ringed the inner edge, as well as the floral arrangement hanging above.

The shiny white dance floor was painted with the bride's and groom's names inside a heart and lit with a spotlight from above, and a six-foot-tall heart made of red roses hung behind the band. I noticed the band members setting up on the stage and mentally checked them off my list. I saw John Farr up on a ladder at the corner of the dance floor and waved to him.

"What do you think?" Mack asked as he sidled up to me.

"It's something," I said, giving his thick arm a squeeze. "The bride is going to love it."

"That's what we want. Do you want to see how the escort card display turned out?" He jerked his head toward one corner, and I followed him.

Buster stood holding a handful of clear plastic arrows with red and pink paper attached to the ends to look like feathers. He turned toward me to reveal a Lucite heart-shaped target on a Lucite easel with at least a hundred arrows protruding from the surface. Each arrow, like the ones in his hand, had paper feathers on the ends with names and table numbers written on them. The color of the papers ranged from the palest pink to fuchsia to light red to crimson.

"It looks exactly like you described," I said, marveling at the display that would tell guests where to sit throughout the room.

Buster placed one of the remaining arrows into the clear heart. "They're arranged alphabetically from left to right and top to bottom, but it still may take people a while to figure it out."

"Either Kate or I can stand next to it and explain the concept," I said, knowing that wedding guests got easily overwhelmed, especially after a cocktail or two.

"Sometimes I wish we could stay for the party and see people's reactions when they walk into the room," Mack said.

Buster placed the last arrow and rocked back on his heels. "Not me. I'm fine leaving all the madness behind and taking a few hours off until we have to return to break it all down."

"I think the cake designers have the best job," I said. "They walk in, set up the cake, and leave. They don't even have to come back because their creation gets eaten."

Mack shuddered. "I don't think I could bear to think of guests eating what I'd worked on for days. Speaking of cake, is Alexandra doing this one?"

I shook my head. "She couldn't fly over this weekend. Luckily a red velvet cake covered in white fondant hearts isn't too complicated to pull off, so we found someone else to make it." I looked across the room and spotted the four-tier cake between the sweetheart table and the dance floor. "I miss having her around, and I know I'm going to miss nibbling on the sugar petals she puts around her cakes."

Our go-to cake baker had relocated to Scotland a few years back when the Type-A DC brides got to be too much for her. Now she only flew in to do cakes for our clients.

"It looks like this room is ready to go," I said. "Are the bouquets still down here or up with the bridal party?"

"Still down here," Buster said. "Maybe he can help you carry them upstairs."

I followed Buster's gaze and twisted to see Richard hurrying toward me. He wore a neatly tailored peacock-blue suit with a pale-yellow shirt open at the collar. Was this how he dressed on a casual Saturday, or had he always intended to crash my wedding? Either was entirely possible.

"There you are," he said when he reached me. "I've been searching high and low. Thank heavens Kate pointed me in the right direction." He swiveled as if noticing his surroundings for the first time. "So this is where red dye number two came to die."

I gave him what I hoped was a withering look, but he ignored it. "I told you the bride was obsessed with Valentine's Day."

"I thought you had a hard-and-fast rule against theme weddings after that *Lord of the Rings* wedding debacle where someone actually forgot the rings," Richard said.

"Compared to the groomsmen having to dress like hobbits, I thought the ring issue was minor," I said. "This wedding didn't start out as a theme wedding, though. It began as a light motif."

"And morphed into something that Hallmark might find to be too much," Richard said.

"Are you here to critique or help me?" I asked, and before he could answer, I tugged him by the sleeve over toward where Mack stood.

The burly florist waved an arm at the white boxes against the wall. "I didn't want to deliver the bouquets without explaining."

I knelt down as he lifted the top off the biggest box to reveal a large heart-shaped bouquet made out of red roses clustered tightly together. "That doesn't need much explanation. That's for Amelia."

"Correct." Mack replaced the lid and lifted the one off another box. "These are for the bridesmaids."

Richard and I looked down at the pink-and-white bouquets nestled in tissue paper.

Mack held up a finger. "They look identical but they're not."

I leaned over to get a better look. Each cluster of pink roses and white hydrangea looked identical to the one next to it. "I give. How do I tell them apart?"

Mack lifted one out of the box. "Amelia had us wrap each one with a special charm that the girls pulled from her cake at the bridal shower. I pinned the name of the bridesmaid on the ribbon wrap so you'll know which one goes to which."

"So even though they look identical, they aren't interchangeable?" Richard asked.

Mack gave a quick shake of his head. "No. She wants each girl to get the right charm. It may look like you can switch them out, but she'll know the difference."

I stared down at the flowers that looked identical from the top but had one small difference. "I can't believe I didn't think of this before."

"Bridesmaids charms are nothing new, darling," Richard said. "Have you never used them before?"

"Not that." I closed my eyes and tried to block out the noise of the band doing sound checks and the waiters filling the water glasses. "It never occurred to me that an identical one could have been substituted without anyone noticing."

"We aren't talking about bouquets anymore, are we?" Mack asked.

I opened my eyes. "Nope, but I think I know how the killer was able to get the poison into the truffle after Richard delivered the box."

❧ 29 ❧

Richard looked at me then at the bouquets in the box then back at me. "You know how the killer put poison in the chocolates just by looking at the bridesmaids' flowers?"

"Tell me something," I said. "Were the heart-shaped boxes you ordered custom?"

He tilted his head at me. "I didn't have time to order the custom boxes, so I went with the heart-shaped boxes they were pushing for Valentine's Day. Why does that matter?"

"Don't you see? Anyone could have gotten an identical box and carefully poisoned the chocolates without having to steal it from Marcie's office. That was one of my big stumbling points. The box was seen on her desk from the time you delivered it until she gave it to her assistant."

Mack snapped his fingers. "But if someone got an identical box and did all the poisoning ahead of time, they'd only have to switch out the box."

Richard put one hand on his hip and tapped his toe on the carpet. "But my boxes had a personalized tag."

"Which they could have easily slipped off and onto the new

box without being noticed," I said. "Someone saw you deliver the chocolates, saw the name of the chocolatier on the top, bought an identical box, poisoned it, and switched it out later."

Richard gave me a sideways glance. "That seems like a lot of effort."

"Not if you'd been waiting for the perfect opportunity," I said.

Mack stroked his goatee. "So it had to be someone at *Capital Weddings*."

This didn't help Cassandra's case any. "Or someone who visited *Capital Weddings* anytime after you did." I didn't want to discount the possibility of another suspect, although the redhead had the best combination of motive and opportunity.

"So how can we know if your theory is right?" Mack asked.

Richard held out his phone. "I'll call the team over at Fleurir. After I placed such a huge order, they adore me."

"Even after you were the reason they were named in the paper connected to a poisoned chocolate death?" I asked.

Richard hesitated then shook his head. "Even then. Money talks, darling."

He took a few steps away from us as he pressed the phone to his ear, nodding as Kate passed him on her way toward me.

"How did it go with Maxwell?" I asked Kate once she'd reached me.

She put her hands on her hips. "Room shots and close-ups of the ceremony and cocktail areas are done. I checked them off the list as he went."

"He must have loved that."

We made it a rule not to micromanage our vendors on the wedding day with the theory that no one did their best work that way. In this case, however, there was the possibility that Maxwell might take out his ire at us on the bride and her wedding photos. Even if Amelia had driven us crazy, there was no way we were going to let that happen.

"I even made him show me some of the images in the view screen just to be sure he wasn't pretending to take the photos,"

Kate said. "I didn't think that was the case, but you never know."

"Good thinking." I knew Kate wasn't being neurotic for nothing since we'd hired a photographer once whose big selling point was that she still shot with film. The only problem was she had a limited amount of film, so she only pretended to take some images, and we ended up with missing details and almost no candids.

"He seems to have gotten over our visit yesterday," Kate said. "He even invited me over to his place for drinks after the wedding."

"Maxwell never disappoints," I said. "I wonder what he'll think if his latest lady love gets arrested for murder?"

"You're assuming Cassandra is his only lady love. Maxwell strikes me as a man who multitasks when it comes to dating."

Kate was one to talk. She had a spreadsheet to manage her upcoming Valentine's Day dates, but I decided not to remind her of this fact.

"You were right, Annabelle." Richard joined us as he slid his phone into the inside pocket of his jacket. "Someone came in the same day I delivered the chocolates to Marcie and showed them a photo of one of my gift boxes and asked for an identical one."

Kate held up a palm. "Wait, what?"

"Annabelle came up with a theory that the killer got an identical box of chocolates and poisoned that one instead of the one he delivered," Mack said.

"Our biggest issue with this case seemed to be how the killer poisoned the chocolates after they arrived at the magazine when no one noticed them leaving Marcie's desk," I explained.

"So a decoy box?" Kate nodded slowly. "Pretty clever."

"I called the chocolatier and happened to talk with the clerk who waited on the woman who wanted an exact copy," Richard said.

"It was a woman?" I asked. "Was the clerk sure?"

"He seemed sure," Richard said. "He told me he didn't get a

good look at her because she wore a long coat with the collar flipped up and both a scarf and knit hat."

Kate leaned on Mack's arm as she stepped out of her black heels. "And he didn't think that was suspicious?"

"Not since it was freezing outside," Richard said. "And before you ask, the woman paid in cash."

"Of course she did," I muttered. "At least we've eliminated Marcie's ex and Maxwell."

"Which leaves us with Cassandra," Kate said.

"There's still Brianna," I argued, although I knew our nemesis was more of a wishful thinking suspect than anything else.

"Let's hope your crackerjack detective boyfriend can get a confession out of her," Richard said. "You did say he was going to talk to her today, right?"

I nodded. "He doesn't know about the copycat chocolates though. Maybe I should call him and let him know. It's information that could be helpful during an interrogation."

Richard whipped out his phone so fast it made me think of a quick draw gunman in the Old West. "I'll do it. I'm the one who talked to the clerk, so I can give him the most accurate information."

"Be my guest." I dropped my phone back into my pocket. "Kate and I need to get the personal flowers delivered and finalize the ceremony setup. Guests should be arriving within half an hour."

Kate pulled her wedding day schedule out of her pocket. "Divide and conquer? You do the flowers and I'll handle the ceremony?"

Mack glanced at Richard pacing as he talked on the phone a few feet away. "I can help you carry the flower boxes up to the bride's suite."

Buster joined us. "When do you want the escort card display out in the foyer?"

"Not until after the ceremony," I said, eyeing the elaborate Lucite heart jammed with clear arrows. "I know they're only plastic, but I don't want people armed with arrows too early in the evening."

Mack's eyes widened. "We didn't think of that. You don't think this is a liability, do you?"

Kate stepped back into her shoes and winced. "Speaking as someone who's attended more than my fair share of weddings where there was a serious injury or death, I don't think the fake plastic arrows are the most deadly thing here."

That made Mack's face look even more alarmed as he looked around the ballroom, no doubt wondering what could be more dangerous. Since we'd run into corpses at more than a few weddings, Kate and I had begun including potential methods of murder in our event troubleshooting plans. Even though we'd thought of at least a hundred ways to kill someone with items at a wedding, I suspected we'd only scratched the surface.

"Don't terrify the creatives," I said to Kate. "And don't forget that the ceremony programs are stashed in the vendor room under my coat."

She gave me a thumbs-up.

I picked up the lighter of the two boxes and balanced it on one hip. "Another visit to the bridal suite will give me a chance to make sure Fern hasn't gone off the rails again with the hair. I don't know if I can handle any more surprises."

"Then you won't like this," Richard said, his face somber as he rejoined us. "The murder suspect Reese went to talk to?"

"Cassandra?" Kate asked.

Richard took a deep and dramatic breath. "She's missing."

❧ 30 ❧

"Tell me again," I said as Mack and I led the way down the corridor to the bride's suite with Richard hurrying behind us. "What exactly did Reese say?"

Richard let out an impatient breath. "I told you already. He went to this Cassandra woman's apartment and she was gone, and her roommate said she'd packed her things and left in the middle of the night."

"That doesn't sound normal." Mack shifted the flower box he held high on one shoulder.

"No, it doesn't," I agreed. "It sounds like something a guilty person does."

"Or a scared one," Mack said.

"Scared of being arrested maybe." Richard took one end of the flower box I carried. "She must have known things weren't looking good for her when you and Kate caught her with Maxwell."

I paused in front of the slightly ajar door to the bridal suite. "Did Reese say anything else?"

Richard cocked an eyebrow at me. "You mean did he whisper sweet nothings in my ear for me to pass along to you? No."

"That's not what I meant and you know it." I let go of my side of the box, and Richard struggled to keep it from falling as I pushed open the door and led the way into the suite.

"Flower delivery," Mack called out, making his usually gravelly voice almost melodic.

Several bridesmaids rushed out of the bedroom, and I was pleased to note they were fully dressed and their hair was done up in classic French twists. The only flourish Fern had allowed himself was what appeared to be rubies tucked into the hair, which actually made a pretty contrast with the pink chiffon floor-length dresses.

Mack lifted the lid off his box and began pulling out bouquets, toweling off the stems at the bottom, and calling out names. The girls ooh-ed and ah-ed as they were handed their bouquets and saw the silver charms dangling from the pink satin ribbon wrapped around the stems.

Richard lowered his box onto the couch and shot me a look, which I made a point of ignoring.

"How's the bride?" I called out to Fern, hearing him fussing over her in the next room.

His head appeared in the doorway, and I noticed there were now tiny rubies decorating his man bun as well. "Wait for it." He disappeared into the bedroom again, and moments later Amelia walked into the living room.

The bridesmaids all ooh-ed and ahh-ed some more. I remembered the gown from the final fitting—a blush pink tulle skirt that belled out with a wide black bow trailing down the back and an appropriately named sweetheart neckline with long tulle sleeves. A dramatic look for a DC bride, but a welcome change from some of the simple to the point of bland gowns I'd seen.

My eyes went to her blond hair, and I let out an audible sigh of relief when I saw it arranged in a loose bun of soft curls at the base of her neck. I decided not to comment on the glittering rubies tucked into the curls and arranged in the shape of a heart. Compared to the other possibilities, this was positively subtle.

"You look gorgeous," I told Amelia, giving her a mostly-air hug.

Richard handed her the heart-shaped bouquet. "Stunning, darling."

Amelia looked confused for a moment, and I suspected she was trying to figure out who he was and why he was handing out bouquets.

"He's with me," I said. "This wedding is so important to us we added extra staff."

That seemed to make her happy and she beamed at Richard, who muttered something under his breath about me not being able to afford him.

"I can't wait for you to see everything downstairs," I said, gathering up her long train.

Her smile faded. "Is it time?"

"It's time to move you all downstairs to the holding room," I said. "The ceremony starts in fifteen minutes."

Amelia began to breathe quickly. "I can't believe it's here. We've been planning for so long." She grabbed one of my hands. "I don't know if I'm ready."

I recognized the panic in her eyes and took both of her hands in mine, speaking in my most soothing voice. "Of course you are. You're marrying a great guy. You look beautiful. You're surrounded by all your friends. It's going to be perfect." I gave her hands a squeeze. "You have nothing to worry about. I'll be with you the entire time."

She nodded and managed a weak smile. "Okay, let's do this."

Fern bustled up, his arms filled with the veil and what looked like small angel wings. "I'll add the veil to your hair right before you walk, sweetie." He pivoted to face the bridesmaids. "Alright, tramps. Follow me."

Mack looked at me, and I remembered that he'd rarely seen Fern in action with the bridal party, which meant he wasn't used to the risqué nicknames. I'd been equally horrified the first time I'd heard Fern talking to bridesmaids until I'd realized that the women thought it was hilarious. Somehow Fern's trash talk cut the wedding day tension and last-minute jitters.

Fern took his place at the front of the procession, waving a hand behind him. "Annabelle, you bring the blond tart."

Amelia giggled, and Mack gasped.

I passed off the train to Richard who spluttered behind the mass of tulle but followed behind the bride as I held her hand all the way to the elevator.

When we'd managed to jam everyone--including Mack--into the elevator car, Fern began giving last-minute instructions to the bridal party.

"Remember, girls. When you walk down the aisle, it's boobs out and bouquets held below your waist by your--"

"Why don't we wait until we're lined up?" I suggested as the door pinged open.

Fern shrugged, thrusting his hand with the can of hair spray high as he led the row of bridesmaids out of the elevator and toward the meeting room where they'd be waiting until all the guests were seated. "This way, hussies."

I was glad there were no guests nearby to hear him, although I did notice a few guests walking into the ceremony and one potential wedding guest in a coat trying to look into the reception ballroom. I hated guests trying to get sneak peeks before the rooms were ready, so as soon as I got the bride settled, I'd deal with the interloper.

Once we were in the meeting room, I handed Amelia off to Fern, who immediately began fussing with her hair and unfurling the veil. I noticed the flower girls in feathery white dresses standing with women I assumed were their mothers.

"You didn't say there'd be children," Richard whispered in my ear.

"Didn't you hear us talking about the cupids? Well, those are the cupids."

Richard backed out of the room, his eyes not leaving the little girls.

"Oh, for heaven's sake," I called after him. "They're three-year-olds, not rabid dogs."

"Then you don't know three-year-olds," Richard said.

"I'll be back to get you all in a few minutes," I told Fern as I slipped out the door and waved at Richard to follow me into the ceremony room.

"I must say, Annabelle," he said as we stepped into the small ballroom. "You managed to calm that bride down with just a few words. I felt sure she was about to burst into tears."

"Practice. I'm used to calming down hysterical people."

He pressed a hand to his chest. "I hope you aren't referencing me, darling."

"Of course not," I said, and I could tell he didn't know whether I was being serious or not.

"Programs are down, lights are tested, string quartet is all set up," Kate said, joining us at the back of the ballroom as I eyeballed the rows of powder-pink chairs stretching in front of us. Heart-shaped programs sat on each chair with paper cones filled with red rose petals tied to the backs of them. I recognized the instrumental version of "My Funny Valentine" and flashed back to the hours Kate and I had spent coming up with love-themed songs for the ceremony prelude music.

"Good work," I said as I took in the altar area.

Buster and Mack had designed an impressive ceremony arch groaning under the masses of pink roses and white hydrangea. A curtain of orchids strung on translucent wire created the back-drop, with a crystal chandelier hanging from the middle of the canopy.

"You don't think you're hammering this Valentine's Day theme a little hard?" Richard asked.

"It's not us," Kate said. "You know Annabelle and I don't go in for themes. Annabelle hasn't even celebrated Valentine's Day in three years."

"Thank you, Kate."

"Anytime," she said, not picking up on my sarcasm. "Although this year she has a hot boyfriend, so who knows what she'll be doing tomorrow?"

"This is not the time to talk about my Valentine's Day plans," I said, hoping my blush was hidden by the room's dim lighting. "We have a bride to get down the aisle."

Kate pulled out her schedule and flipped a page. "The groom and groomsmen are ready. I pinned on the boutonnières and made sure the best man has the rings."

"Please tell me the men aren't wearing pink tuxedos," Richard said.

"Black," Kate told him. "Ralph Lauren single breasted three button."

Richard gave a small shrug. "Acceptable."

"With boutonnieres of pink-and-red tea roses backed with heart-shaped leaves," she added.

Richard made a face. "Unacceptable."

I smiled at a pair of arriving guests and pulled Kate and Richard further away from the entrance. "It's a little late to redo the look. Why don't you two corral all the guests into seats while I help Fern with the cupids?"

We walked out of the ceremony room and split up. I gave the foyer area a cursory glance for guests trying to sneak into the reception ballroom but didn't see anyone.

"Annabelle!"

I turned to see Sidney Allen rushing up to me. His face was mottled pink, and his temple beaded with sweat as he tried to keep his headset from slipping down. He hiked his black suit pants up around his armpits when he reached me.

"Is everything okay?" I asked. Although the entertainment designer was known for being a bit of a control freak and a diva--not unusual character traits in my business--I'd never seen him so wound up on a job before.

"This is a travesty." His words came out in staccato bursts as he gasped for breath between them. "My number one dove team called in sick. Bird flu. Can you believe it?"

I actually couldn't. "I don't think birds get the flu, do they?"

He swiped a hand across his sweaty forehead. "Who knows?

The handler had them cough into the phone on the message, but I don't think it was the birds at all. I think he was faking. Anyway, I've had to call in my second-string doves."

"Okay," I said. "That doesn't sound so bad. Doves are doves, right?"

He recoiled from me and sucked in air. "Wrong. My prima doves can fly in a heart-shaped pattern like we'd planned. I don't know what these birds can do. Flap their wings? Caw? Who knows? I hate working with second-tier performers. I just pray they don't poop on everyone's head."

That made two of us.

"Calm down." I took him by the shoulder. "No one but us and the bride know about the heart-shaped flight pattern. If it doesn't happen, it doesn't happen. It's not worth having a coronary over." I immediately regretted my choice of words.

Sidney Allen looked stricken. "You know I had to leave my Leatrice for this, and now it's a disaster. It serves me right for abandoning my lady love in her time of need."

"Leatrice is fine," I said. "Prue is over there right now with the baby and Hermes. Nothing bad is going to happen to her. I promise."

Sidney Allen blinked up at me. "She is? They are?" His shoulders relaxed. "Thank you, Annabelle. That makes me feel better." He took a shaky breath. "I'd better go sort out these ragtag birds."

I watched him hurry off and crossed my fingers that the doves weren't as dodgy as he claimed. I didn't relish the idea of cleaning bird poo out of guests' hair all night. I felt a buzzing in my pocket and retrieved my phone, smiling when I saw Reese's name on the screen.

"Richard told me about Cassandra," I said when I answered. "Do you have any idea where she could have--"

"Babe," my boyfriend interrupted. "I'm not calling about her. I discovered something about Marcus."

❧ 31 ❧

"**W**hat about Marcus?" I held the phone to my ear as the doors to the ceremony room opened and the sound of the strings playing "Love Me Tender" drifted out.

"Remember how he was arrested and kicked out of college before graduation?"

"Yes," I said. "What does that have to do with the murder case?"

"Maybe nothing," Reese said, the sounds of car horns in the background telling me he was driving. "I like to know as much as I can about the victims, even the ones we think may not have been the intended victim, so after Richard told us what he'd found, I thought it might not hurt to do a bit more digging. Turns out there was a witness in the case that placed another person in the stolen cop car with him."

"Okay." I wasn't sure where he was going with this.

"That other person disappeared or ran away," Reese said. "Long story short, they didn't get caught or charged with a felony like Marcus did."

"And Marcus never mentioned the other person?"

"I read the transcript from his questioning, and he claims he acted alone."

I turned and walked toward the other end of the foyer away from the snippets of music. "So if there was a second person, Marcus covered for them and took the fall for everything himself."

"One more thing," Reese said. "The witness who saw the other person claims it was a woman."

My mind raced. "Are you thinking what I'm thinking?"

"If you're thinking that the other woman could have been his best friend from college and the woman who gave him a job when no one else would, then yes, I'm thinking what you're thinking."

"This means that Marcie had a significant motive to get her old pal out of the way," I said. "Especially if he was as loose-lipped as everyone claimed. She couldn't risk him revealing her part in a crime when she was in a position of importance."

"I'm guessing she's been steering us in the wrong direction from the beginning so that we'd think she was the intended victim," Reese said. "It was pretty clever."

"But what about Cassandra?" I said more to myself than to him. "She made a run for it. Doesn't that mean she's guilty?"

"Maybe it means she figured out who killed Marcus or figured whoever killed Marcus might come after her. I'm guessing she ran because she was afraid. Not because she was guilty."

"Did Richard tell you about the decoy box of chocolates?" I asked, watching a few guests hurry into the ceremony room.

"Decoy box?" Reese sighed. "He didn't put it that way, but yes."

Kate waved at me from the ceremony room door and tapped her wrist. It was go time. "I have to get a bride down the aisle, so I'd better run." I spotted a guest loitering next to one of the tall planters outside the doors to the reception ballroom. "As soon as I scold this guest for trying to get a peek at the reception room."

"I love it when you get tough," Reese said with a chuckle.

"Then you're going to love this," I said, shaking my head as I watched the person stick their hands into the dried moss around the base of the tree. "I'm going to have to ask someone to stop rummaging around in the foliage."

"I don't even know what that means."

"Excuse me," I said, holding the phone down so I didn't yell at Reese at the same time. "I'm going to have to ask you to leave the trees alone and go inside for the ceremony."

The person glanced up at me, and I nearly dropped the phone. "Marcie? What are you doing here?"

Even though she wore a long wool coat and a scarf wrapped over her hair, the editor was easily recognizable. She pulled something out from the moss and tucked it inside her coat then took off running.

"Get back here!" Even though she'd hidden it quickly, I recognized the item she'd dug out of the planter—a heart-shaped chocolate box.

Kate and Richard stepped out of the ceremony ballroom as Marcie ran by them, Kate's eyes widening as she recognized the magazine editor.

"Stop her," I yelled as I took off running, still holding my phone.

Kate kicked off her shoes and joined me, running down the stairs to the lobby. I heard Richard in the background screaming about the ceremony, and I screamed back that he and Fern were in charge.

Marcie was already out the glass doors when we reached the ground floor, and we flew past the doorman who looked startled to see three women running, two of them in black cocktail dresses. She made a left onto the boardwalk, dodging pedestrians and pushing people out of her way.

Kate pulled ahead of me and was only a few feet behind her when Marcie hung a sharp right down the long dock extending into the river. My side ached but I didn't stop running. Not when the killer was getting away with the evidence. She looked over her shoulder at us and ran even faster. When we'd almost reached the end of the dock, I slowed. There was nowhere to go but out into the Potomac River or back toward me, so I braced myself to tackle her when she reversed course. To my surprise, she jumped up onto the railing and leapt into the water.

Kate skidded to a stop and leaned over to peer into the river. "She jumped."

I ran up and joined her at the railing, watching Marcie below us in the frigid water. "I can see that. Where does she think she's going?"

"With that wool coat on?" Kate said. "No place but down."

We watched as she struggled to stay afloat. People had begun to gather with us at the railing, murmuring as her head disappeared under the water, reappeared, and went under again.

"Someone should go in after her," I said.

"I hope you aren't looking at me," Kate said. "That water is freezing and this dress is silk."

I saw a flash as another person jumped into the water and then saw Reese's head pop up with Marcie in tow.

"Where did he come from?" Kate asked, looking over her shoulder.

"I ran into him outside the hotel and pointed him in the right direction," Richard said, walking briskly up to us but not running.

"I thought you were back handling the ceremony," I said, glancing at the towering hotel behind him.

"And miss all the fun?" Richard asked. "Never. I left Fern to get the bridal party down the aisle."

Kate gave a low whistle. "Thank goodness we hired a videographer for this wedding. I can't wait to see how that went down."

"I'm sure he did a fine job," I said, trying to convince myself more than anything.

A pair of burly firemen ran past us and proceeded to hoist Reese and Marcie out of the water.

"I also may have called 9-1-1," Richard said with a shrug. "It seemed like an emergency."

Kate tugged the neckline of her dress lower. "You know I'd never say no to the fire department."

"Is there anything you would say no to, darling?" Richard asked, giving her his most saccharine smile.

Kate ignored him and headed toward the flashing lights of the fire truck on the boardwalk.

Once Reese was out of the water and had a blanket around his shoulders, I rushed up to him. "What were you thinking jumping into the Potomac like that?"

"I thought you'd gone into the water," he said, his teeth chattering as he spoke. "Everyone on the dock was yelling about the women jumping in the river. I figured you'd gone in after Marcie."

I wrapped an arm around him even though he was soaking wet. "Nope. Kate and I were arguing about who should save her when you jumped in."

He managed a laugh. "That makes more sense." He held up the soggy heart-shaped box. "And, of course, I did save the evidence."

"That must be the decoy box of chocolates," I said.

"And if my guess is right, this is the one Marcus ate from and all the chocolates are poisoned," Reese said, turning the wet box in his hands.

I squeezed him. "Thanks for wanting to save me."

He gazed down at me and water from his hair dripped onto my face. "Anytime, babe."

I stood on my tiptoes to kiss him, and even though his lips felt cold, kissing him still sent a current of warmth through my body. The sound of Richard clearing his throat made me pull away.

"I hate to break this up, but one of you has a wedding to run, and the other has a wet criminal to process."

"He's right," I said. "I need to get back to the wedding."

Reese looked over at Marcie, who was also wrapped in a blanket but looked furious as two firemen were holding her tightly. "And I have a killer to interrogate."

A big part of me wished I could be at the interrogation instead of at the wedding. "You know I'm here until midnight."

He kissed me one last time. "I'll wait up for you at home."

Another throat clearing from Richard. "I don't mean to be a

nuisance," he said pointing to the fire truck, "but if we don't get Kate now, she very well may ride off with the cute firemen."

I looked to where Kate sat in the driver's seat of the fire truck with a shiny red helmet on her head.

Reese laughed as I let out a long weary breath. "You can't ever say your job is dull, babe."

He was right about that.

32

"I finally chased down that ring bearer who went rogue with his bow and arrow," Fern said as he strode into the room and plunked a small white bow and a quiver filled with white feathery arrows onto the table.

We were all taking a break after making it through the ceremony, cocktail hour, and bridal party introductions, and were seated around a banquet table in one of the smaller meeting rooms set aside as a break room for wedding vendors. A long table filled with trays of sandwiches, pasta salad, and cookies ran along one side of the room with a smaller table at the end that held a silver bowl filled with ice and a selection of bottled waters and sodas.

"Where's the errant ring bearer now?" Kate asked, propping her bare feet up onto a chair.

"I put him in a time out," Fern said. "Those arrows may be plastic, but you try getting shot in the rear with one."

"Next time we'll make them without points," Mack said to Buster as he filled a plate with pasta salad.

"I'd hoped the arrow motif was a one-time thing," Buster said.

"I don't know." Kate shook her head. "People were pretty impressed by the escort card display with all the arrows in the

Lucite heart target, and just wait until the photos appear in a magazine."

"If this becomes a trend, I may need to find a different profession," Fern said, touching a hand to his backside.

I stifled a laugh. "Thank you again for running the processional without us. I'm sorry you got shot in the process."

Fern fluttered a hand at me. "It's not your fault, sweetie, although I might ask that in the future we don't arm the youngest members of the wedding party. I'm just lucky I had my scepter."

Since Fern had singlehandedly gotten the bridal party down the aisle, I'd decided not to mention his use of the contraband scepter, especially since it sounded like it had been useful in corralling the flower girls and ring bearers.

"Now that we can take a breath, do you want to explain what happened?" Fern asked as he sat down. "One minute you were there and the next you were running out of the hotel and Richard screamed at me to start the processional."

"I wouldn't say 'screamed,'" Richard said from where he stood at the buffet table examining the food. "Kate had cued the string quartet, so the bridesmaids' song was already playing. I had no idea how long it would last, so I assumed time was of the essence. I merely prodded you to get the bridesmaids down the aisle."

Fern mouthed the word 'screamed' behind Richard's back.

"Well, it seems to have gone off without a hitch," I said, twisting the cap off a mini bottle of Coke. "The bride didn't say a thing when she recessed up the aisle."

"I told her you were both fluffing her train and wouldn't let her look behind her," Fern said. "She had no idea you weren't in the hotel."

Kate gave him an appreciative nod. "Good work. I don't know if I could have sold that one."

"It helped that the rogue ring bearers were a distraction and that the oldest flower girl dragged one of them down the aisle in a headlock," Fern said with a giggle, then stopped when he saw my expression. "The little tyke was fine, of course."

"I'm just glad the hard part is over," I said. "On both accounts. The killer is in custody, and Amelia is officially married."

"Explain to me again how you and Reese figured it out," Mack said, putting his heaping plate down on the table.

Richard cleared his throat. "I do believe my information was crucial in the process."

"It definitely steered us in the right direction to confirm that the killer bought an identical chocolate box the same day Richard delivered his to the *Capital Weddings* office," I said.

Kate swung her legs down from the chair. "The most confusing part of the case was trying to figure out how the poison could have gotten into the truffle and why someone would poison just one of them. It didn't make sense."

"Until we realized that there had been a second box of chocolates, and the second box was the one that was poisoned," I said.

"But that box wasn't the one Marcie gave to her assistant?" Buster asked, leaning his forearms on the table.

I shook my head. "Nope. I suspect she offered him a poisoned chocolate sometime earlier, probably when it was just the two of them, then she gave him the other box later to pass out to the staff."

"Which explains why there was more than one truffle's worth of chocolate in his stomach, but the staff swore up and down that he only ate one." Kate stood up and walked to the cookie tray. "And why it appeared that the killer was after Marcie because they poisoned the one she would have eaten."

"She was clever about it," I said. "She laid clues to make us think the poisoned chocolate was meant for her. I'm sure she broke the lock on her office door herself to make it look like someone was after her and to make it look like the killer had access to the box of chocolates that she left on her desk."

"When really she poisoned the truffles at home and brought in the tainted box the next day," Richard said.

Mack shook his head and swallowed a mouthful. "She went to a lot of trouble."

"I think she realized what a liability her old friend was after she hired him." I took a sip of Coke. "We now know she probably owed him big time if he took the fall for her back in college, but she must have resented having that hanging over her head."

"And everyone mentioned that he liked to gossip," Kate said, picking two chocolate chip cookies and handing one to me. "She must have assumed that he'd eventually let something slip and she could get fired."

Richard took the seat next to me. "Depending on the statute of limitations, she could even be charged with that old crime."

"Those are certainly motives to kill someone," Fern said. "I've known Potomac wives who knocked off their husbands for less."

We all stared at him.

"What?" He shrugged. "I mean, I can't know for sure, but I do have a lot of widows for clients. There can't be that many rich men with dodgy hearts."

Kate nibbled on the edge of her cookie. "He makes a good point. Rich men do seem to have more heart attacks."

"I still don't get how you connected it to Marcie," Mack said. "Unless you didn't know until you saw her today."

"And why was she searching our planters?" Buster asked.

"To be honest, we still thought Cassandra was the killer until Reese decided to dig deeper into Marcus's past," I said. "When he called me and told me about the second person at the scene of Marcus's felony, we knew it had to be Marcie and that gave her a serious motive. I wasn't 100 percent sure until I saw her pull something out of the bottom of one of your trees."

"How did she get the decoy chocolates into one of Buster and Mack's trees?" Kate asked. "It doesn't make any sense."

"I don't know for sure," I said, "but I think she had the poisoned box in her bag when she came to Love Brunch the day of the murder. She probably knew the offices would be searched, so she brought it with her intending to dump it somewhere. Maybe she forgot until she saw the cops, but she must have stashed it under all the moss and planned to retrieve it later."

Kate slapped the table. "That's why she was at the hotel the other night. Not to talk to her ex. She thought those trees were part of the hotel's regular decor."

"And we told her they weren't and also told her where they'd be the next day for our wedding," I said. "So she showed up looking for the box she'd hidden, because she knew someone would stumble upon it sooner or later."

"Unfortunately, Annabelle spotted her before she could make a clean getaway," Richard said.

Fern spread his arms wide. "And the rest is history."

My phone buzzed and I pulled it out, feeling a flutter of nerves when I saw my boyfriend's name on the screen.

"So?" I asked when I answered. "Did she confess?"

Reese laughed. "No hello?"

"Don't toy with me," I said in my sternest voice. "We're all here dying to know what happened."

"Yes, she confessed. It took a while, but once I outlined all the evidence we had against her and maybe exaggerated a little, she broke down."

I put my hand over the mouthpiece. "Marcie confessed."

Everyone cheered and clapped.

"She said she'd been planning to kill Marcus, but when Richard delivered the box of chocolates, it gave her the perfect fall guy," Reese said. "She already had the liquid nicotine and had been looking for a way to put it in his food, so it didn't take her long to get the decoy box, add poison to all the truffles, and switch out the boxes. Even though the box got soaked, the lab will still be able to test all the truffles and confirm they're all filled with nicotine."

"How many did he eat from the poisoned box?" I asked.

"About half. Plenty to give him a deadly dose."

"And she watched him eat them?" I shuddered. "Talk about coldhearted."

"Not very much in keeping with the Valentine's Day spirit," Reese said.

"Don't worry," I said. "We're making up for it with this wedding. I am officially OD'ed."

"I hope not, babe. The holiday isn't until tomorrow."

My stomach clenched. In all the wedding chaos and murder investigation, I'd gotten nothing but a card for him. I was officially the worst girlfriend ever.

"I'd better go," Reese said. "I still have a mountain of paperwork before I can head home. I'll see you later tonight."

"Is everything okay?" Kate asked, pulling out her schedule. "You have a look on your face like we forgot something big."

"Funny you should say that," I said. "I forgot to get Reese something for tomorrow."

Fern gasped. "You didn't go to The Pleasure Chest like I suggested?"

"I did not," I said. "I don't think a first Valentine's Day calls for leather and chains." I gave a nod to Buster and Mack. "Present company excepted of course."

Both men blushed.

"Don't worry, darling," Richard said with a curt wave of one hand. "I've got the perfect idea."

"This should be good," Kate said under her breath. "If you need backup, call me and I can bring over some leather and chains."

I glanced at the clock on the wall and walked to the boxes of candy we'd lined up against the wall. "Ready to set up the candy station?"

Kate rubbed her hands together. "Perfect timing. I ran out of my stash of gummy bears a half hour ago."

I pulled open the flaps of one of the cardboard boxes and my stomach dropped. It was empty. I ripped open the next one and found the same thing. Kate rushed over and we opened every box to find them all empty.

"It was Brianna," Kate said, pointing to the door in the back of the room used by service staff to come and go without being seen by guests. "I wasn't losing my mind. I *did* see her. She must have snuck in through the back corridors connected to the kitchen."

I couldn't believe it. Brianna had taken out the bags of candy inside and refolded the tops of the boxes so they looked untouched.

"She knew you wouldn't open them until later," Richard said.

"When it was too late to do anything," I added, my mouth dry.

"It's never too late," Mack said. "If she came in through the loading dock, she had to exit through it, and our trucks have been down there for hours."

The two florists hurried out of the room as Kate and I stood side by side in shock.

Fern joined us as we stared down at the empty boxes, resting a hand on each of our shoulders. "This means war, ladies."

❧ 33 ❧

I rubbed my eyes and sat up, taking a few seconds to remember I was in my own bedroom. "What day is it?" I mumbled to myself.

The wedding the day before had seemed to stretch on forever, and I recalled dragging myself home and Reese tucking me into bed. I'd been too tired to hear about his interview with Marcie or to tell him about the rest of the wedding. I glanced at the rumpled sheets next to me. Speaking of my hot-cop boyfriend, where was he?

I flopped back down onto the pillows and draped an arm over my eyes. The way the sun streamed into the room between the slats on the blinds, I knew it had to be midmorning. I rolled my head to one side to look at the alarm clock and did a double take. Almost noon? I'd slept half the day away.

I swung my feet over the side of the bed and groaned as they touched the rug. Everything still hurt from being on my feet for over twelve hours. I spotted my black cocktail dress with pockets--one of my wedding day uniforms--in a heap on the floor and vaguely remembered stepping out of it before collapsing into bed.

What I needed was a shower, I told myself as I stood up. And maybe a handful of ibuprofen.

At least the wedding had ended up being a huge success complete with a candy display, I reminded myself. Buster and Mack had been right about the loading dock. Almost all of the bags of candy had been abandoned, and we suspected Brianna had given up trying to haul them all when she couldn't get her car into the loading dock because of the Lush trucks blocking the way. She'd gotten away with some of the candy, but we'd salvaged enough to create an impressive display.

A clattering sound stopped me on the way across my bedroom and told me Reese was still here. I opened the door and paused. More clattering sounds, and with the door open, I could smell the rich aroma of coffee and the savory smells of breakfast. Reese wasn't much of a cook, but whatever he'd whipped up--or ordered in--smelled amazing. The shower would have to wait. I stopped by the bathroom just long enough to swish some toothpaste around in my mouth and down a pair of Advil tablets before continuing down the hall.

Was Reese really singing while he cooked? I'd never known him to do either. I leaned my head into the kitchen and blinked hard, convinced I was seeing double. Not one, but two dark-haired men wearing aprons stood at the stove.

"Well look what the cat dragged in," Richard said, putting one hand on his hip and waving a wooden spoon at me. "What's this look, darling?"

I glanced down at the T-shirt Reese had put me in last night and realized it was one of his navy-blue DC Metropolitan Police T-shirts that only reached mid thigh on me.

Reese came over to me and rested his hands on my hips. "I think it looks good on you, babe."

"What's going on?" I managed to ask as I took in the kitchen counters covered with grocery bags, cutting boards, and bowls.

"Your boyfriend wanted to cook you a special brunch for Valentine's Day," Richard said, waving his spoon more. "But since he doesn't know how to cook, he called in an expert."

"I hope this is okay," Reese whispered, pulling me closer. "I didn't want to make you wake up and get dressed up after your wedding, so I thought I'd do something for you here. I didn't want to get takeout again, and I can't really cook so . . ."

"I think it's incredibly sweet," I said, knowing that for Reese to willingly spend the morning being bossed around by Richard was a sacrifice in and of itself.

Richard poked his head between us. "I'm not just creating brunch, I'm teaching Mr. Biceps here how to cook." He winked at me. "My gift to you, Annabelle. After this at least one of you will be semi-functional in the kitchen."

"I may have bitten off more than I can chew," Reese said, looking over his shoulder at Richard, who'd gone back to his place at the stove. "He's a bit of a taskmaster."

I raised an eyebrow at him. "You're just figuring that out now?"

Richard tapped his spoon on Reese's shoulder. "Back to work, Loverboy. We still have these soufflés to get into the oven."

I inhaled deeply and caught whiffs of cinnamon and sugar. "Are you making The Hay-Adams' oatmeal soufflés?"

When Richard smiled at me, I was surprised not to see canary feathers peeking out of his mouth. "I sweet-talked the recipe from their head chef with the promise not to use it for my catering." His face clouded for a moment. "Not that I have much of a business left." He gave his head a curt shake. "But none of that today."

I bit back the urge to remind Richard that his business wasn't ruined, especially since the real person who poisoned the chocolates had been caught. I knew that talking about it would only whip him into a frenzy.

"Thank you," I said to Richard, who nodded but didn't look at me.

"Don't mention it, darling. Besides, my significant other is away on another work trip so what else did I have to do?"

I looked around the floor for his tiny dog. "Where's Hermes?"

"He had a sleepover with your downstairs neighbor," Richard said. "They were in the middle of a Matlock marathon last night, so I let him stay."

"How is Leatrice?" I asked, knowing both men had seen her more recently than I had.

"You'd never know anything happened to her," Reese said. "When I came in last night, she met me at the door and had heard all about the call to the harbor already."

"I guess Sidney Allen didn't have any luck hiding her police scanner."

"Enough about the old girl." Richard waved me away with both hands. "You need to get out of the kitchen and let the boys finish up."

Reese rolled his eyes but turned his head so Richard wouldn't see him. "It shouldn't be too much longer. There's champagne in the living room."

I stood on my toes and gave him a quick kiss. "You thought of everything."

Richard coughed.

"You both thought of everything," I corrected, letting go of Reese and heading toward the living room.

I stopped when I saw the setup and blinked away tears. They *had* thought of everything. The dining room table had been cleared of the usual piles of paper and set with white china and pale-pink stemware. A tall arrangement of sandy-pink blooms I recognized as Sahara roses--my favorite variety of rose--centered the table with a single rose tucked into the blush-pink silk shantung napkins folded on each plate. A silver champagne bucket, chilling a bottle of bubbly, stood beside the table, and a carafe of orange juice sat next to a tray heaped with croissants. At the top of one of the plates, I saw a small box tied with red ribbons and topped with a tiny envelope, my name written in calligraphy on it.

How many favors had Reese, or Richard, pulled in? The flowers had to have come from Buster and Mack--no other florist knew my favorite type of rose. Not only did I owe them big time for finding the stolen candy, I owed them for delivering my favorite flowers on their busiest day of the year. I looked at the box, recognizing the name of the Georgetown jeweler, and my heart began to race. This wasn't a proposal setup, was it? I looked down at the man's T-shirt I wore and put a hand to my messed-up hair. Even if Reese thought proposing to someone half comatose was a good idea, Richard would never allow it. Would he?

I pushed the idea from my mind. It was way too early to be thinking of marriage. We'd just moved in together. The topic hadn't even come up. Only a crazy person would propose before feeling out the situation, right? I reminded myself that even if Reese was impulsive, Richard was not. He would never go along with a scheme that involved me getting engaged in anything less than full makeup and potentially a designer outfit.

I saw two glasses of champagne pre-poured on the coffee table beside a bowl of strawberries and another of whipped cream. I took a sip from one of the glasses and was about to dip a strawberry into the whipped cream when my apartment door flew open.

"Does anyone have triple A batteries?" Fern stood in the doorway wearing a headset and holding a Lucite clipboard. His usually pristine hair was pulled back in a low ponytail, but several dark strands had slipped out and hung in his face.

"Are you okay?" I asked. I'd witnessed Fern juggle the most demanding bridal parties with ease, but at the moment he looked like a hairdresser on the edge.

"Kate's gone off schedule." He waved the clipboard in the air. "Her brunch date was supposed to end at noon so we could do a refresh and change outfits for her late lunch date, but I can't reach her." He tapped the earpiece of his headset. "I think Sidney Allen's equipment is malfunctioning or out of batteries."

"Let me take a look." I walked over to him and eyed the headset.

"You're a lifesaver, sweetie." He took the champagne out of my hand. "Don't mind if I do."

I watched as he downed the bubbly in a single gulp. "I think the headset's working fine. Your problem is probably Kate."

He handed me the empty glass. "What do you mean? She has the schedule. Why won't she respond?"

"Kate is great with schedules for wedding days, but you know how she is when it comes to men. She loses track of time when she's really into someone."

Fern's jaw went slack. "I've made a terrible mistake. I added the new boy--the fireman she met yesterday--in for brunch. I should have put him in the late-night slot instead of the lobbyist. She never would have gone overtime with a lobbyist."

"Don't beat yourself up too much," I said. "I'm sure Kate will turn up soon."

If the fireman was as cute as I remembered him to be, soon was a relative term.

Fern thrust the clipboard at me. "Here. You take over. I can't handle the stress of planning. How do you do this every weekend?"

Richard walked out of the kitchen with two plates. "What are you doing here?" he asked Fern. "This is not a communal brunch."

Fern's face lit up when he spotted the berries and cream. "But you're here."

Richard pulled himself up to his full height as he set the plates down on the dining table. "I am the chef. You need to leave before you spoil the romantic mood I worked so hard to create."

"There you are." Kate walked in behind Fern. "Why did you go AFH?"

"What's AFH?" Fern asked.

"Away from headset," Kate said, shrugging off her pale-pink coat and draping it across my couch to reveal a short red sweater dress that was more formfitting than some of my underwear. "I've been talking to dead air for ten minutes."

Fern pressed the side of the headset and his cheeks flushed. "I must have accidentally turned it off. What happened with the fireman?"

Kate rolled her eyes and picked up the other full glass of champagne from the coffee table. "Turns out he already had a girlfriend, and she texted him during brunch."

"Ouch," Fern said, taking the clipboard back from me. "That does put us back on track for lunch with the lawyer though."

"All's well that ends well," Richard said, trying to shoo them out with his oven mitts. "You two can discuss your strategy in the hall."

"I'm not so sure about this plan," Kate said, dodging Richard's mitt and swigging the champagne. "I may be going about this love thing all wrong."

"Obviously," Richard mumbled, "but is now really the time to discuss it?"

Reese appeared with a mug and handed it to me as he appraised the scene in the living room. "You might need this."

I wrapped my fingers around the mug and breathed in the scent of coffee and chocolate. By then I was more than awake, but the warmth was welcome, especially since it didn't look like I'd be getting my hands on champagne anytime soon.

Reese looped an arm around my waist. "Maybe brunch at home wasn't the best plan."

"I'm sure Richard will clear them out in a second," I said, leaning into him and taking a sip of the hot mocha.

"Mike?" A deep voice from the hall made everyone turn around.

"What's your brother doing here?" I asked.

My boyfriend cringed. "Dropping off tickets. Part two of the Valentine's Day plan. I forgot to tell him not to interrupt part one." He waved an arm so Daniel could see him. "Over here."

I looked up at him. "Tickets?"

"I was supposed to pick them up yesterday but it got a bit crazy, so Daniel swung by and got them for me. I wanted to have them for you this morning."

Fern wiggled his eyebrows at me. "The show was my idea. You're going to love it."

Daniel made his way past Richard, who was trying to shuffle

everyone toward the door, and handed an envelope to his brother. He gave the apron a second glance but just smirked.

I was always struck by how much my boyfriend's older brother looked like him--only with a touch of gray at the temples. Nice to know Reese men aged well.

"Daniel," Kate said as she ducked by Richard. "Are you here for brunch?"

Daniel smiled at her and shook his head. "I'm on my way out. You're all dressed up for something."

Kate gave him a playful swat. "This old dress? Do you like it?"

"You'd look pretty in a garbage bag," he said.

Kate leaned one hand against his chest. "Aren't you sweet? You sure you don't have any plans for today?"

Another head shake. "A walk by the Potomac and coffee at Baked and Wired."

She hooked her arm through his. "Throw in a cupcake and it sounds like the perfect day."

Daniel grinned at her. "Deal."

Fern gaped as the pair walked out of my apartment arm in arm. "What about the schedule? What about the dates? Who's going to tell the lawyer or the lobbyist?" He threw the clipboard over his head and it landed on the couch. "I need more champagne."

"I hope it's to toast with," Leatrice said from the doorway.

"Oh, for the love of everything holy." Richard slapped an oven mitt to his forehead. "Not her too."

"Leatrice," I said, "what are you doing out of bed?"

She stood next to Sidney Allen and both wore red flannel pajamas covered with hearts. It felt odd to see the entertainment diva in anything but a suit. Luckily, he'd hiked the pajama bottoms up around his armpits, so the look wasn't a complete deviation.

Leatrice held out her hand and fluttered her fingers. "I had to show you this."

Fern staggered back a few steps. "Are you engaged?"

Leatrice bobbed her head up and down as Sidney Allen puffed out his chest. "He proposed this morning."

I felt tears prick the back of my eyes as I watched my elderly neighbor beaming with happiness. "That's wonderful. Congratulations!"

"We don't need to tell you who we'd like to plan our wedding," Leatrice said.

Fern rushed forward. "Of course I'll do it, sweetie. You don't need to ask me twice."

Leatrice looked stunned as he threw his arms around her and Sidney Allen and pulled them inside.

"I'm sure we'll all help," I said, walking over and giving her a hug of my own.

"Sit," Fern said. "I want to hear all about the proposal, and then we need to start brainstorming about the wedding." He gave Leatrice the once-over as he pushed her onto the couch. "I'm thinking we take your hair pink."

Reese grabbed the jewelry box from the table, lifted the bottle of champagne from the standing wine bucket, and took me by the hand into the hall, closing the door behind us. He sat on the top step of the staircase and plopped me onto his lap. "That's better."

"Richard won't be happy when he realizes we're not in there," I said.

"We can go back in a second. I just want a quiet moment before you have to start planning Leatrice's wedding." He handed me the box wrapped in red ribbons. "Happy Valentine's Day, babe."

My throat felt dry as I untied the bows and lifted the lid off the box. A single diamond drop necklace glittered up at me.

"I did think about getting you a heart-shaped necklace, but Richard told me you might be scarred by hearts after the wedding you just planned."

"It's perfect," I said, finding my voice and holding it out for him to put it on me. I lifted my hair as he fastened the clasp. "I love it."

He touched a finger to the diamond as it rested in the hollow of my throat. "And I love you." He kissed me softly at first and then more deeply, wrapping his arms around me and pressing my body against his.

When we came up for breath, I felt dizzy. "Your gift is inside, but I don't think I should go inside to get it right now. I can tell you what it is."

"You didn't have to get me anything," he said.

"It's nothing this fancy," I said, running a hand along the chain of the necklace. "I got you cable so you can watch the games here and you don't always have to go to a bar or your brother's place. The plan with the sports package."

He threw back his head and laughed. "It's perfect. I love it."

"And I love you," I said, grinning at him. I glanced down at the envelope his brother had given him. "So what show are we going to see? Aside from the one going on in our apartment?"

"Open it." He handed me the envelope. "Fern did this part. He swore up and down you'd love it."

I pulled out a pair of tickets and squinted at the print. "The Burlesque Circus. I didn't know DC had burlesque."

Reese took the tickets from me. "He was supposed to get Miss Saigon." He shook his head slowly. "This is what happens when I outsource."

"To be fair, Fern probably thought Miss Saigon was a drag name." I took the tickets back and studied them. "Is it a drag burlesque?"

Reese started laughing and buried his head into my neck, his body shaking. "I can't wait until the guys at the station find out I'm going to drag burlesque shows."

I kissed his neck. "Who knows? You may like it."

He tilted his head to meet my lips, using one hand to pull my head closer as he deepened the kiss. He pulled back and smiled at me, his eyes half-lidded. "I really hope not."

Before we could kiss again, our apartment door opened and Richard appeared holding two champagne flutes. He marched out and handed them to us. "You're going to need these."

"Thanks, Richard," I said to his back.

"I'll be back with your first course," he called over his shoulder. "There is no way this brunch is going to waste, and I'm not letting that riffraff inside eat it."

The door slammed shut, leaving us in the relative quiet of the stairwell.

"Thanks for being cool with all of this," I said as I readjusted myself on Reese's lap. "Not every guy would be okay with my crazy friends."

"I've always known it was a package deal, babe."

"A crazy package," I said.

"That's putting it mildly," Reese said then shrugged. "It's the strangest thing, but as infuriating as they can all be, I can't imagine life without them."

I threw my arms around his neck. "That's exactly how I feel."

THE END

The Hay-Adams Hotel's Oatmeal Soufflé

1 cup whole milk
2 tablespoons butter
¾ cup quick rolled oats
1/3 cup cream cheese
½ cup light-brown sugar
½ teaspoon salt
¼ teaspoon nutmeg
½ teaspoon cinnamon

3 large eggs, separated
½ cup and ¼ cup granola, divided
8 blueberries
8 raspberries
Softened butter, as needed for ramekins
Sugar, as needed for ramekins

Set the oven to 325 degrees. Prepare 4 medium ramekins (about 4½ inches diameter) by brushing the interiors with butter, then dusting with sugar.

In a small saucepan over medium heat, bring the milk and butter to a simmer. Slowly add the oats and cook, stirring with a spatula, until thick, about 3 to 4 minutes. Remove from the heat. Add the cream cheese, brown sugar, salt, nutmeg, and cinnamon and stir until smooth. Stir in the yolks from the 3 eggs and ½ cup of the granola. Let the batter come to room temperature.

In a medium mixing bowl, whip the 3 egg whites to stiff peaks. Fold them into the batter and divide the batter in half. Fill each ramekin halfway with batter, then add 2 blueberries and 2 raspberries to the center of each soufflé (don't let them touch the sides). Dust each soufflé with 1 tablespoon of granola. Top with the remaining batter and bake 35 to 40 minutes, until the soufflé has risen and the top isn't soft. Serve immediately.
(Serves 4)

This recipe appeared in the October 2017 issue of Washingtonian Magazine.

LEAVE A REVIEW

Did you enjoy this book? You can make a big difference!

I'm extremely lucky to have a loyal bunch of readers, and honest reviews are the best way to help bring my books to the attention of new readers.

If you enjoyed *The Truffle with Weddings*, I would be forever grateful if you could spend two minutes leaving a review (it can be as short as you like) on Goodreads, Bookbub, or your favorite retailer.

Thanks for reading and reviewing!

ACKNOWLEDGMENTS

As always, an enormous thank you to all of my wonderful readers, especially my beta readers and my review team. I never give you enough time, but you always come through for me. A special shout-out to the beta readers who caught all my goofs this time: Linda Fore, Bill Saunders, Sheila Kraemer, Sandra Anderson, Linda Reachill, Kaitlyn Platt, Tricia Knox, Annemarie Pasquale, Linda Fore, Tony Noice, and Christy. Thank you!!

A heartfelt thank you to everyone who leaves reviews. They really make a difference, and I am grateful for every one of them!

A special shout-out to the show *Death in Paradise*. I got the idea for the switcheroo box of chocolates from one of their episodes. I love watching mysteries as well as reading them and get ideas from everywhere!

ABOUT THE AUTHOR

Laura Durham has been writing for as long as she can remember and has been plotting murders since she began planning weddings over twenty years ago in Washington, DC. Her first novel, BETTER OFF WED, won the Agatha Award for Best First Novel.

When she isn't writing or wrangling brides, Laura loves traveling with her family, standup paddling, perfecting the perfect brownie recipe, and reading obsessively.

She loves hearing from readers and she would love to hear from you! Send an email or connect on Facebook, Instagram, or Twitter (click the icons below).

Find me on:
www.lauradurham.com
laura@lauradurham.com

CPSIA information can be obtained
at www.ICGtesting.com
Printed in the USA
LVHW031918010420
651904LV00001B/174